WITHDRAWN

DISTANT THUNDER

DISTANT THUNDER

STUART WOODS

RANDOM HOUSE
LARGE PRINT

Copyright © 2022 by Stuart Woods

Penguin Random House supports copyright. Copyright fuels creativity, encourages diverse voices, promotes free speech, and creates a vibrant culture. Thank you for buying an authorized edition of this book and for complying with copyright laws by not reproducing, scanning, or distributing any part of it in any form without permission. You are supporting writers and allowing Penguin Random House to continue to publish books for every reader.

All rights reserved.
Published in the United States of America by Random House Large Print in association with G. P. Putnam's Sons, an imprint of Penguin Random House LLC.

Cover illustration by Mike Heath

The Library of Congress has established a Cataloging-in-Publication record for this title.

ISBN: 978-0-593-63261-1

www.penguinrandomhouse.com/large-print-format-books

FIRST LARGE PRINT EDITION

Printed in the United States of America

1st Printing

This Large Print edition published in accord with the standards of the N.A.V.H.

This book is for Martha Snowman.

DISTANT
THUNDER

1

STONE BARRINGTON WOKE to the loudest explosive noise he had ever heard, and there was more to come. Lightning flashed, illuminating his bedroom at his house in Dark Harbor, Maine, then a hammering on the roof began. He switched on a bedside light. It came on for a moment, then went off for a few seconds, then he heard the generator kick in, and the lamp came on again.

Holly Barker came running into the room; he had not even noticed her absence. She dived into bed and clung to him. "Please tell me this is a thunderstorm and not a nuclear attack," she whimpered.

"It's the mother of all thunderstorms," Stone

said, then switched on the TV to the Weather Channel. A man stood before a weather chart, and there was a large red splotch on it where Maine should have been.

"It's a nor'easter," Stone said. "Last night they were saying this would come in the night, then pass offshore. I think it's making itself at home."

"I am not flying in that little jet of yours today," Holly said.

"Nobody is. You can tell them at the office that you have a real good excuse for not showing up. You can refer them to the weather radar."

"What's that terrible noise on the roof?" Holly asked.

"That's called rain."

"That's not like any rain I've ever heard on any roof," she said.

"The Weather Channel guy was predicting eight to twelve inches of rain in our neighborhood."

"Is your airplane going to be okay?"

"Fortunately, it's waterproof. And yesterday, Seth drove stakes into the ground and tied it down, so it won't blow away."

"You were expecting this?"

"No, but Seth was. He's a Mainer. He put extra lines and fenders on the boats, too."

"Look out the window. It's as though we are underwater."

"We are, in a way."

"Why haven't we lost power?"

"We have, but our 25 kW generator kicked in, and that keeps the whole house running."

"For how long?"

"Until that five-hundred-gallon tank of diesel runs out, and that will take a long time."

"How long?"

"I don't know."

They put on robes and went down for breakfast. Seth's wife, Mary, was putting food on the table as if nothing unusual had happened. "Morning," she said cheerfully.

"Morning, Mary," Stone replied. "How many days of provisions do we have stocked?"

"Oh, don't you worry about that, Mr. Stone. We won't starve. Good thing we have that twenty pounds of moose in the freezer that Mr. Rawls gave us last year."

"Moose?" Holly said. "Last year?"

"Ed Rawls goes moose hunting every year," Stone said. "He has a hard time getting rid of the meat."

"What's moose like?" Holly asked.

"I haven't the slightest idea, and I thought I was never going to find out, but one never knows, do one? As Fats Waller used to say."

"Who's Fats Waller?"

"Oh, you child! A large, brilliant pianist, songwriter, and singer of the 1920s and '30s."

"I hope you don't think I remember the 1920s and '30s."

"You don't remember World War II, either, but it happened. So did Fats Waller."

They devoured scrambled eggs and sausage and Wolferman's English muffins, washed down with orange juice, and followed by black coffee, an espresso roast.

Seth lit the living room fire, though it wasn't all that cold; it just seemed that way. Stone and Holly showered together, as usual, and got into some L.L. Bean clothes. As they came downstairs, the doorbell was ringing. Stone opened it to find a suit of bright yellow waterproof clothing, topped by a seaman's hat, a thick moustache, and round glasses.

"Come in, Ed," Stone said to Rawls. "What the hell are you doing out in this?"

"Helping to divert a minor disaster," Rawls said. "The ferry got sideways and had to be realigned."

It was late in the Labor Day holiday weekend, and the "folks from away," as the Mainers call them, had abandoned the island yesterday, in a rush. This happened every Labor Day, not just when there was a nor'easter.

"I hadn't heard."

"Nothing to worry about now. I had a look at the airfield. Your aircraft is still attached firmly to the ground."

"Always good news. Anybody hurt in the foofaraw?"

"No. And only one murder."

"Who got murdered?"

"No ID yet. He was found on the ferry deck. The state police won't venture out until this storm has gone."

"Cause of death?"

"Two in the head," Ed said, as if there were one every week.

"That does not bode well," Stone said.

"Not for him, anyway."

"Have you got a description?"

"A medium-everything white gentleman, clad in yellow oilskins, like everybody else."

"Not somebody looking for you, I hope." Rawls was retired CIA, the last of his breed on the island, and there had been times when people had wanted him dead, but not recently.

"We'll just have to see, won't we? I hope it ain't too early for me to want a drink."

Stone got him a bourbon on the rocks.

"You ain't joining me?" Rawls asked reprovingly.

"Not for another eight hours, or so."

Holly came downstairs. "Hey, Ed."

"Hey, Holly."

"I was eavesdropping on the stairs and heard your conversation."

"Then I got nothing else to report. You were flying back today, weren't you?"

"Well, gee, Ed."

"Yeah, I know."

"I've got to check in now and deliver the news."

"It's being delivered in D.C. right now," Rawls said, "so it won't come as a surprise to them at the White House."

Holly was President of the United States and found she had some business in the Northeast for the past few days.

She went to the hidden office that Stone's cousin, Dick Stone, had built for himself to stay in touch with CIA headquarters. Holly had had her own computer installation hooked up. She sent messages to all who needed to hear about the weather in Maine.

2

AT LUNCHTIME, the weather was unchanged. Ed Rawls was pressed into staying for some lobster stew, and they all sat down at the dining table.

"I like to brag on the weather to those from away," Rawls said, "but they're never going to believe this."

The doorbell rang, making them all jump. Stone, clutching his napkin, got up and went to answer it. A man in the usual yellow oilskins stood there, identifiable only by his campaign-style, flat-brimmed hat. "Good afternoon, Stone," said Sergeant Young of the Maine State Police.

"That's an outright lie," Stone said. "Come in and get dry." He pointed at the pegs where the sergeant's gear should be stowed. "We've got a big pot of lobster stew," he said. "Can I tempt you?"

"You can," the sergeant said, hanging up his oilskins and sitting down at the table.

"I think you know everybody."

The sergeant nodded at everyone.

"I've heard bad news from the ferry," Stone said. "Got an ID yet?"

The sergeant reached into his jacket pocket, produced a wallet, laid it on the table, and opened it. Everybody at the table recognized the CIA credentials. Everybody stopped eating.

"Name of John Collins," the sergeant said. "Anybody know him?"

Heads were shaken.

"Anybody heard of him?"

"Give me a minute." Holly set down her spoon, picked up the wallet, and went to the concealed office and her computer. Inside, she dialed a number.

"Lance Cabot."

"It's Holly."

"I thought you would have drowned by now."

"Near enough. Do you know one of your people named John Collins?"

"Perhaps," Lance said.

"Is he supposed to be in Maine?"

Lance was quiet for a long moment. "How bad?"

"Fatal."

"Means?"

"Two to the head. Happened on the ferry, which hasn't run since last night."

"Perhaps you'd better stay there for a while."

"Where else am I going to go?"

"I know you're due back in New York. Don't go."

"I can't swim that far."

"Has the state police become involved?"

"The island-based Sergeant Young is at Stone's lunch table as we speak."

"I don't want them to have the body."

"Nobody can move it in the present weather."

"Ask the sergeant to move it to Stone's garage at the first opportunity, then to call me on this line. You stay where you are and watch your ass." Lance hung up.

Holly returned to the table. "That was Lance Cabot on the phone. You're about to have another guest, Stone; one John Collins, says Lance. Sergeant," she said, handing him a note. "Please call Lance at this number as soon as you're able. He asks that you not remove the body from the island but store it in Stone's garage."

"So now I'm running a mortuary?" Stone asked.

"Looks like it. They won't be able to get a chopper in here today."

"I'll have to call my captain," the sergeant said.

"If I know Lance, he's doing that right now. Call him before you speak to your captain." The sergeant's cell phone rang. He walked away from the table and answered it, then returned. "Stone, you have an ice machine, don't you?"

"Two of them."

"Can I borrow some plastic garbage bags and all your ice?"

"Leave enough to fill a few whiskey glasses," Stone replied.

The sergeant nodded. "Somebody from our station told me that we're going to get more rain here this weekend than we've had since the hurricane of '47. That one was about nineteen inches, as I recall."

"Stone," Ed Rawls said, "if we get that much rain, your two boats down at the dock are going to end up on your back lawn."

"As long as they don't end up in my living room," Stone said.

After lunch, everybody had a glass of whiskey, because there wasn't anything else to do. Around nightfall, the sergeant's colleagues deposited the remains of John Collins in the garage, next to Stone's MG TF 1500, with bags of ice around him. Stone and Holly both had a good look at him.

"Know him?" Stone asked.

"No," she said, snapping the man's photo with her iPhone. "But Lance might."

3

STONE SLEPT LONGER THAN USUAL, and so did Holly. He got up and looked out a window: it was still raining, but not as much, and occasionally, a bit of blue sky could be seen. He switched on the TV, muted it to let Holly sleep, and looked at the weather radar. "Oh, good," he said to himself.

Stone was at breakfast when Holly came down, dressed, but looking a bit bleary. "What's happened?" she asked, sitting down. "Why is the rain gone?"

"Are you complaining?" Stone asked.

"No, just disoriented. I've grown accustomed to wind, rain, and thunder."

"God changed his mind. Live with it." He sipped his coffee. "We may be able to fly today."

"Lance said I can't go back to New York," she said.

"Where does he want you to go?"

"He wants me to stay here, until he says I can return to Washington."

"I guess I can stand one more day here," Stone said, "but tomorrow we're flying or you're enjoying Maine on your own."

"There's a reason he doesn't want me to return yet."

"What reason?"

"He didn't say. But Lance never gives suggestions without a reason. Has anybody checked on John Collins?"

"Still dead, and Seth has refreshed his ice packs."

"Good."

"Which part?"

"The ice packs."

"You said Lance knows Collins?"

"He said he does, but he may not."

"Either I'm confused, or Lance is."

"What I heard on the phone yesterday was Lance being baffled. He told me he may know Collins, because he doesn't want us to know he doesn't know him."

"Now I'm baffled," Stone said.

"Lance cultivates an air of knowing everything."

"I've noticed that," Stone said.

"Sometimes, if he doesn't, he pretends to. When we next hear from him he will have had time to find out what he doesn't know. I sent him the photograph of the corpse. Maybe that will help him order his mind."

They heard a distant ringing.

"That's the phone in the little office." Holly got up and trotted in that direction. She had been spending a couple hours a day tending to White House business and dealing with various issues.

"Hello?"

"It's Lance."

"Good morning."

"Is it? Has the torrential rain gone away?"

"Sort of. Have you learned anything new about Mr. Collins?"

"I have. Mr. Collins doesn't exist."

"That's fairly obvious. I mean, he hasn't complained about the ice."

"You misunderstand. There is no one by that name employed by the Agency in any capacity. I ran the photo you sent through our identity recognition software, which is the best in the world, and he apparently doesn't exist anywhere."

"Has that ever happened before?"

"Early on, when we were still getting the bugs

out of the software, but not recently. There is no record, anywhere, of his fingerprints, either."

"I didn't send you his fingerprints."

"The Maine State Police did."

"Shall we return the corpse to them? It's technically in their custody, anyway."

"They'll send a chopper down as soon as they can. In the meantime, keep him iced."

"Don't worry."

"You can come back to Washington tomorrow. I'll tell the Cabinet to expect you."

"Fine."

"You may be interested to know that Islesboro has had twenty-one inches of rain during the last two days. It's a record."

"I'll alert the media, such as they are."

"They already know. I read it in the Bangor newspaper."

"You're a subscriber?"

"We subscribe, in one way or another, to every news source in the world."

"I had forgotten."

"For shame." Lance hung up, and Holly went back to the table and reported the news to Stone.

AT MIDDAY, A police chopper set down at the airfield and an ambulance met them there, the ferry service having been restored. They came to

Stone's house, removed the corpse, then flew it away.

Seth, without being told, disinfected and pressure-washed the garage floor, then left the outside door open to hurry the drying. Mr. Collins was no longer a houseguest.

4

THE FOLLOWING DAY, Stone freed his airplane from its bonds, and since he had only Holly and half the fuel aboard, he got it off the runway in an amazingly short distance and flew back to Teterboro, where he turned the aircraft over to the people in the Strategic Services hangar and Holly over to the Air Force One crew, for transfer to Washington, and he was met by his factotum, Fred, in the Bentley and driven home.

Stone was greeted by his secretary, Joan Robertson, as he walked into his office. "There's little to warrant your attention," she said, "since I have proceeded on the basis that you would not return until the snow flies. You may go back to Maine now, if you wish."

"What a warm and cheerful welcome!" Stone said, scratching the ears of Bob, his Labrador retriever. "At least Bob is glad to see me."

"Lance Cabot called a few minutes ago, to pass on the news that knowledge of Mr. Collins's existence has still not been claimed by any person or organization. No need to return the call."

"Just as well."

"I, however, have a theory about the identity of Mr. Collins."

"I don't suppose I can avoid hearing it, so spit it out."

"I believe Lance knows full well the particulars of the corpse and its history, but he, for purposes of his own, will not admit to any of it."

"That's a theory about Lance, not about Mr. Collins."

"Take it as you will," she said, and flounced out.

"Don't flounce!" Stone shouted after her but didn't get the favor of a response.

Joan buzzed him. "Dino on one."

Stone picked up the phone. "I'm back," he said.

"I figured that out," Dino replied. "Dinner at P.J.'s at seven tomorrow night?"

"You're on." They both hung up. Joan buzzed immediately. "A Mrs. Collins to see you. She doesn't have an appointment."

"Any relation?"

"No idea."

"Send her in."

A tall, slender, and attractive woman in her thirties walked in and offered her hand. "I'm Vanessa Morgan," she said.

"I'm sorry, I was told you were a Mrs. Collins."

"I am the widow of John Collins, with whom I have heard you became acquainted after his death. We have been married for seven years, but since I long ago established myself in the fashion industry under my maiden name, I didn't take his."

"Please sit down, Ms. Morgan."

She did so.

"How can I help you?"

"I wanted to hear directly from you what you know about John's death."

"Not much, I'm afraid. We had a terrible storm in Maine, during which your husband's body was found aboard the island's ferry. The weather prevented his removal to state police headquarters, so they prevailed upon me for the use of my garage, where the body was packed in ice until a helicopter could transport it. I'm afraid that is the limit of my knowledge, but I would like to ask you some questions, if I may."

"All right."

"How was your husband employed?"

"He was an officer of the Central Intelligence Agency, working in the directorate of operations, which is one of the reasons why we didn't see much of each other."

"What were the other reasons?"

"We just didn't get on and didn't enjoy each other's company much. It was always a relief when he was called away."

"Do you know when he first joined the Agency?"

"Two years before we were married. He was allowed to tell me only what I just told you."

"Did he have any other family?"

"They are all dead."

Stone wrote down a number and handed it to her. "You may call a Sergeant Young at this number to arrange disposition of the remains."

"Disposition is all I require of them. He wanted to be cremated and scattered in the sea, if that matters. I plan to honor that."

"Please tell Sergeant Young that."

"All right."

"Do you know who your husband's immediate superior was at the Agency?"

"The only name he ever mentioned to me was Cabot. He didn't mention a first name."

"May I ask, how were you informed of your husband's death?"

"A man came to my door yesterday, saying that he worked for John's employer, then gave me the news and his condolences. He left an envelope with information on how to claim John's insurance and pension."

"And what was that gentleman's name?"

"If he gave one, I didn't get it."

"Can you describe him?"

"About your height and weight; better dressed than I would have expected an Agency official to be. Quite handsome. Early forties, perhaps."

"I suppose that could describe a lot of people."

"I suppose it could, but for the handsome part."

There was a silence, while each of them waited for the other to speak.

"Is there anything else I can do for you?" Stone asked, finally.

"I don't know," she said. "Is there?"

"May I ask, how did you come to seek me out?"

"Your card was in the envelope the gentleman from the Agency gave me. Do you know why?"

"I do some consulting work for them, and I was present in Maine at the time of . . . the event. I can't think of any other reason."

She gathered herself to leave.

"Ms. Morgan?"

"Yes?"

"In your conversation with the gentleman from the Agency, do you remember whether the words 'in the line of duty' were mentioned?"

"Yes, they were. Why?"

"If he died in the line of duty that might affect the amount of the insurance and pension payments. When you apply, you should mention that on the form."

"A good point," she said. "I thank you for your

assistance. I hope, perhaps, to see you some other time, in more pleasant circumstances." She laid a card on his desk, then turned and walked out.

Joan came in. "Who was that?" she asked.

"That was Mrs. Corpse," Stone replied.

5

THE NEXT NIGHT, Stone, Viv, and Dino sat at the bar at P. J. Clarke's. Stone told them about the Collins corpse.

"John Collins?" Dino asked.

"Right."

"I know that name from somewhere, but I can't remember where or when."

"I'll send your apologies to Rodgers and Hart."

"It'll come to me," Dino said.

"I'll wait with bated breath."

"Somebody asked for him at the bar, before you arrived," Dino said.

"I think that must have been Tom Collins."

"Who?"

"A somewhat out-of-date cocktail. Gin and grapefruit, I believe."

"You're right."

"I usually am," Stone replied.

"Not as often as you think."

"More often than **you** think."

Viv had not spoken since they sat down. "Shut up, both of you," she said.

They did.

"You're worse than women."

"Worse at what?" Stone asked.

"Everything."

"I take exception."

"Take all the exception you like. There's plenty to go around."

"Viv, help us out with this John Collins thing. What's your opinion?"

"I think there's a real good chance he's dead," Viv replied.

"My wife is choosing not to participate in this discussion," Dino explained.

"I got that," Stone said. "Let's order."

They ordered.

Viv looked around. "This is a guy joint," she said.

Dino argued, "I'd bet you there are more women than men here, if I had enough fingers and toes."

"That doesn't mean it isn't a guy joint," Viv said. "A lot of women prefer a guy joint: they think there's a better chance of meeting guys at the bar."

"Guys with joints," Dino said.

"Stop it!" Viv nearly shouted. "Is that what passes for wit around here? No wonder I'm out of the country so much!"

"Well, Dino isn't exactly Noël Coward with the quips, is he?" Stone said.

"You shut up, too!" she said.

"I'm just agreeing with you," Stone said, wounded.

"Normally that's an attractive quality in you, Stone, but not tonight."

"Well, you won't give us your theory on the late John Collins," Stone said.

"All right, here's my theory. First Lance told you that he's aware of Collins, right?"

"Right."

"But then he stated that Collins is unknown to him or the Agency?"

"Right."

"I deduce that, on one of these two occasions, Lance was lying."

Stone broke up. "Dino," he said, "I don't know how you manage a sex life when she's making you laugh all the time."

"If you were having sex with Dino all the time," Viv said, "you'd laugh, too."

Stone threw up his hands. "I'm getting out of this one and staying out." He waved at a waiter for the check.

6

STONE SAID GOOD NIGHT to the Bacchettis at the rear side door, where Dino's car awaited, then he continued through the bar, where he was surprised to see John Collins's widow, Vanessa Morgan, paying her dinner check at the bar.

"Good evening," he said.

"Oh, good evening. I didn't see you earlier," she said. She signed her credit card receipt.

"I was having dinner with some friends in the back dining room," he replied. "Tell me, have you been a widow long enough for me to invite you to have a drink at my house?"

"Of course," she said. "Seeing other people's homes is my business." They walked out the front door, where Fred got her into the Bentley and

Stone followed. "Why is that your business?" Stone asked.

"Because next week a magazine about interior design debuts, and I am its editor. Its name is **Indoors and Out.** I've worked in the fashion business for years, and this is a fashion magazine about décor. All the houses and apartments in the first issue are from homes I've visited."

They arrived at the house, and Stone took her in through the front door. She stood in the living room and looked around. "I can get your house into our second issue."

"Thank you," Stone replied, "but I'm not ready to invite the public into my home." He took her into his study and poured them both a cognac, while she settled into the sofa.

"This is such a perfect room for a bachelor," she said.

"Widower." He told her about his marriage to Arrington Calder and her death.

"My condolences," she said.

"Thank you."

"It's odd that our respective spouses died the same way."

"Sort of," Stone said. "My wife was killed by a former lover. Was there someone like that in John's past who might be the culprit?"

"Perhaps," she said. "Our marriage and his work were such that his time away from me was a blank slate."

"Have you ever met Lance Cabot?"

"Cabot was the surname that John mentioned as his superior. Could that be Lance?"

"Very possibly. He is the director of the Agency, and he very much resembles the description of the man who visited you and left John's insurance and pension papers."

"Would the director of the Agency personally deliver paperwork?"

"He might, to an Agency widow."

"How odd."

"Perhaps not. Lance defines his job to suit himself, or maybe he just happened to be in your neighborhood and wanted to save a stamp."

"It sounds as if you know him well."

"As well as can be expected," Stone said. "As I mentioned to you, I'm a part-time consultant to the Agency, so I've dealt with him a number of times."

"Do you think the Agency is somehow involved with John's death?"

"Since he was an Agency officer, I'd be surprised if they weren't involved somehow. He may have been on a mission for them when he met his end. I have no way of knowing that, of course."

"Of course," she said. "I have experienced conversations ending when the Agency was mentioned."

"Secrecy is their most important tool," Stone

said. "And now, having mentioned the organization, we should end this part of our conversation."

She laughed.

"One last thing: Do you know about the wall of stars?"

"What's that?"

"When an officer dies in the line of duty, a star is placed on a wall near the entrance of the headquarters building at Langley: no name, just a star."

"A package was delivered to me at the office today," Vanessa said. "It contained three medals. No note."

"When an officer is decorated for exceptional duty, his medals are retained until his death. Apparently John excelled on at least three occasions."

"No further details?"

"No."

"No point in asking?"

"No."

"That's very unsatisfying."

"A lot about the Agency is unsatisfying to those who are not on the inside."

"Well," she said, draining her glass. "I have to be bright-eyed and bushy-tailed first thing in the morning."

"I'll have Fred drive you home," Stone said. He walked her to the car, and before she got inside, she planted a soft and inviting kiss on his lips. "Next time, let's start earlier and finish later."

"I'll look forward to that," Stone said. He closed the car door and Fred drove her away.

Stone went upstairs and pressed the button on the security system that closed and locked down the house. As he got into bed, the phone rang. "Yes?"

"It's Lance. Did you enjoy your evening? The latter part, I mean."

"I should tell you it's none of your business," Stone said, "but it wouldn't do any good."

Lance laughed and hung up.

7

STONE WAS AT his desk the following morning when Joan buzzed. "Two gentlemen in suits and ties," she said. "They flashed badges."

"Send them in, I guess."

Joan led two men into his office. Stone looked them over: too well dressed to be NYPD. "Good morning, gentlemen," he said. "What can I do for the FBI today?"

They exchanged glances. "We'd like to ask you a few questions," one of them said.

Stone waved them to seats. "Coffee?"

Both shook their heads.

"Okay, shoot," Stone said, then raised his hands. "Though not literally."

"We believe you are acquainted with a gentleman called John Collins."

"At this point, no one is acquainted with Mr. Collins," Stone said.

The two exchanged another glance.

"We believe he was a guest in your home in Maine a few days ago."

Stone smiled. "Not exactly," he said.

"What do you mean?"

"I mean that Mr. Collins was more the guest of the Maine State Police, and he spent a night on the floor of my garage, packed in ice, awaiting transport to their ME."

They both stared at Stone blankly.

"Were you gentlemen not aware that Mr. Collins is deceased?"

"We were asked to investigate a murder and were given his name simply as a starting point, not as the victim."

"Your superiors really should try to keep up, instead of wasting your time."

"We were wondering why we were asked to investigate a murder, since that is not a federal crime."

"It was in this case, because Mr. Collins was a federal employee. Still, not knowing that he was dead was rather a serious oversight."

"Do you know how Mr. Collins met his death?"

"He was shot twice in the head while aboard

the ferry that runs from Lincolnville, Maine, to the island of Islesboro. There seemed to be some doubt as to when his death occurred. I'm afraid I don't have any further knowledge than that."

"Do you know what part of the federal government employed Mr. Collins?"

"I was led to believe that it was the Central Intelligence Agency."

They exchanged yet another glance.

"For further information," Stone said, "I refer you to Mr. Lance Cabot, director of the CIA. He's at Langley, except when he wishes to be elsewhere. I happen to know that he was in New York last evening."

"And how would you know that?"

"Because we share a mutual acquaintance who would know."

"Who was?"

"I'm afraid that is confidential."

"And where are Mr. Collins's remains?"

"At the bottom of the sea," Stone said. "They were scattered by his widow yesterday, I believe."

"We won't trouble you further, then," one of the men said. "Thank you for your assistance." They stood and left.

Joan came in. "What did they want?"

"They didn't seem to know," Stone replied. "I had to explain it to them."

"Lance Cabot is on one."

Stone picked up the phone. "Lance," he said, "what a surprise!"

"Have you heard from the FBI about our mutual acquaintance?"

"They just left, knowing little more than when they arrived," Stone replied. "And I think 'acquaintance' is a bit of a stretch, when one of the two parties got dead early in the game, a fact of which the two FBI gentlemen had not been apprised by their superiors."

"They never cease to surprise me," Lance said.

"Before you go, Lance, I would be grateful if you would explain why John Collins was in Maine on your instructions and why you don't want anybody to know that."

"I compartmentalize," Lance replied, "and Mr. Collins and everybody else were in different compartments."

"Is there any other information about the man that you would like me to disseminate the next time I'm asked about him?"

Lance seemed to think for a moment. "I believe not," he said, then hung up.

Stone buzzed Joan.

"Yes, sir?"

"Joan, if you should receive any calls from people seeking information about one John Collins, please deny all knowledge of him and hang up."

"Got it," she said.

8

THE NEXT MORNING, Stone had a coffee at his desk and read the **Times.** On a back page, a death notice caught his eye. These were paid advertisements announcing the deaths of people who were not famous or notorious enough to warrant a full-blown obituary by the newspaper. Their purpose, apparently, was to tell people who might have known them that they were deceased. John Collins's announcement appeared without a photograph, and after the recitation of his dates of birth and death, he was described as a graduate of the City College of New York and of NYU School of Law and a civil servant.

Joan buzzed him. "Bill Eggers on one."

Stone picked up the receiver to speak to the managing partner of his law firm, Woodman & Weld. "Good morning, Bill."

"Morning. Did you see the **Times** this morning?"

"My dog brings it to me in bed every morning."

"I mean the thing about what's-his-name."

"It's a big newspaper, Bill," Stone replied. "Can you give me a hint? News, sports, business, crossword?"

"Dead people."

"Ah, the obituaries."

"No, at the bottom of the page."

"Death announcements?"

"That's it, in the little, tiny newsprint."

"I check it most days to find out who I've outlived."

"You knew him, of course."

"I'm sorry, Bill, you haven't zoomed in far enough."

"Jack, ah, Cummings!"

"Bill, do you possess a magnifying glass?"

"Right here, on my desk."

"Apply it to the announcement you're talking about and read me the name."

"Collins."

"Ah, the infamous John Collins."

"He was also at NYU Law. Everybody called him Jack."

"Got him," Stone said, "bottom of the page."

"That's the one. You had to know the guy, Stone. He made quite a name for himself."

"I tend to ignore ones like that. They were always wanting to borrow your notes, or something."

"He kept the whole law school in grass."

"Well, he wasn't afraid of risk, was he?"

"Didn't you ever buy from him?"

"Bill, I don't even smoke cigarettes. I choke if I try to inhale any foreign substance. Sometimes, I vomit."

"**Everybody** knew this guy."

"I didn't meet him until late in life, **very** late in life." Stone gave him the condensed version of that meeting.

"That's crazy. Same school as this guy, then decades later, he turns up dead in your garage!"

"He turned up dead on the ferry. My garage was used to keep him cool and dry until they could airlift him to the morgue. You may recall the rain of last weekend."

"Oh, yeah. Did you get a look at his face?"

"Yes, it was bland and uninteresting."

"Did you see the scar?"

"I must have missed that."

"Two guys tried to steal his stash, and he fought them off, except one of them had a knife. It made the **Daily News.**"

"I've always read the **Times.**"

"You were a snob even then?"

"You wound me, Bill. I never knew you thought I was a snob."

"Of course you're not. Weren't. But some people thought so."

"I was just reserved, I guess, and some people mistook that for being snobbish."

"That sounds right."

"Bill, is there anything I can do to ease your pain on the loss of your college pal and dealer?"

"He wasn't **my** dealer. I didn't have a dealer. He was just everybody's dealer."

"The CIA must have missed that when he applied."

"He applied for the CIA?"

"And was accepted. He was an officer in the operations department at his death."

"Does Lance know about this?"

"I assure you, he does."

"So he just ignored this guy's criminal record."

"I'm not aware that he had a record."

"Well, maybe not, but he should have had one."

"Perhaps Lance knew but regarded it as a mark of Jack's enterprise and found that attractive in a candidate."

"If you say so."

"I don't say so. That was just a wild guess."

"Well, I'd better get going. There's a couple of more people who'd like to hear about this."

"Bill, don't mention Jack's after-school job on the phone. You never know who's listening. You don't want to besmirch his name this late in the day."

"Yeah, right." Eggers hung up.

9

AFTER LUNCH, Stone got up from his desk, used the toilet, then returned, to find Lance Cabot sitting across from him. "Good afternoon," he said.

"Good afternoon, Lance. Have you had lunch? Can we offer you a sandwich?"

"Thank you, no. I had a taco from a street vendor."

"Can we get you a Pepto-Bismol?"

"Not yet. I'll keep you posted. Stone, why didn't you tell me that you and John Collins were friends in law school?"

"Because I learned that he was at NYU only when reading the **Times** death notice this morning. And when he was there, I didn't know him."

"You never bought grass from him?"

"I've never bought grass from anyone—except once, when a girlfriend wanted to bake me brownies, then **she** bought it, and I reimbursed her. Tell me, Lance, why didn't you mention at the outset that not only did you know Collins, but he was your creature?"

"That's putting it rather too strongly," Lance said.

"How many years did he serve in the Agency?"

"Nine."

"Were you his supervisor for all of that time?"

"Most of it."

"Then how was he not your creature? And, to skip down a bit, why did you litter the Maine ferry service and my garage with his corpse?"

"He got himself onto that ferry, and the Maine State Police got him into your garage."

"What was he doing in Maine, if not at your bidding?"

"That's a need-to-know thing, and you do not need to know."

"That's funny, because people are coming out of the woodwork who think that not only do I need to know, but that I **do** know."

"They don't need to know, either."

"Perhaps it would be best if I just dictated to Joan an account of my experience with Officer Collins and let her distribute it to the press, the wire services, and whoever comes into my office."

"That would compromise an important operation, now running."

"Why? Most of what I know and a few things I didn't know were published this morning in the **New York Times.**"

"All right, what do you want to know?"

"Everything I don't already know."

"I'm not ready to brief you on that operation yet."

"Do I have that to look forward to, or should I just deny all knowledge of Collins?"

"It's not necessary for you to deny all knowledge."

"You may tell me these things in confidence, then I would be bound by the attorney-client privilege."

"Whose attorney are you?"

"Yours and, willy-nilly, Mr. Collins's."

"I suppose you are, aren't you?"

"Asked and answered, a condition that does not extend to you."

"I will answer you when I can."

"You mean, when it's convenient."

"That, too."

"Now, tell me why you are in my office, declining my sandwiches and my Pepto-Bismol."

"I was in the neighborhood," Lance replied.

"Why don't you take a stroll in the Turtle Bay Gardens, out back? It's lovely this time of year."

"Why?"

"Then I can lock the door behind you."

"I have your key," Lance said.

"Why did I give you a key to my house?"

"You didn't. I fabricated it."

"May I have it back, please?"

"No. I may need to get in on another occasion."

"Is someone pursuing you?"

"Usually," Lance replied. "Ah!" He cupped a hand to his ear. "I hear my car. I'll go now." Then he did.

Stone was going to tell Joan to lock him out, then he recalled that it wouldn't do any good.

10

STONE AND VANESSA MORGAN met in the reception room at Patroon, then found Dino and Viv already at their table. Introductions were made.

"Funny," Dino said to her, "I thought your last name would be Collins."

"I declined that opportunity at the time of our marriage," Vanessa replied.

"As many women do," Viv said, "though not I."

"Any more questions related to Collins," Stone asked, "before we put that subject aside permanently?"

"Thank you, Stone," Vanessa said.

"Don't mind Dino," Stone replied. "He's a policeman, and he feels he has a God-given right to know everything about everybody."

"Are you saying that I don't have that right?" Dino asked.

"I am."

"Then you're under arrest, and I'm taking you in for further questioning."

Everybody laughed.

"See what I mean?" Stone said. "And he's known me for twenty-odd years."

"Yes, and they've certainly been odd," Dino reposited.

"I can't promise you that it won't be like this all evening," Stone said to Vanessa.

"What kind of policeman are you, Dino?" she asked. "Do policemen specialize, like doctors in a hospital?"

"Many officers should repose in the psychiatric wing," Stone said.

"Are you including Dino in that group?"

"Certainly not. I'd never hear the end of it. And since Dino is being shy about answering your question, I will tell you that he is the police commissioner of New York."

"And I specialize in everything," Dino added.

"That means that there is no one's business that Dino's nose wouldn't be stuck into."

Mercifully, a waiter appeared and they gave their drinks orders and accepted menus.

"Viv, what do you do?" Vanessa asked.

"I'm a retired cop, and now I work for

Strategic Services, the world's second-largest security company."

"Don't ask which is the largest," Stone said. "You'll never get a straight answer."

"We never speak its name," Viv said.

"See?"

They all ordered the chateaubriand and a big plate of onion rings, and a Caesar salad to start. Stefan, the headwaiter, did his conjuring act with the Caesar and served them from a giant wooden bowl.

"I hear Lance visited you today," Dino said to Stone.

"Oh, he wanders in and out, when he doesn't have anything else to do, which is often."

"Did everybody see John's death notice in the **Times** today?" Vanessa asked.

"Yes, did you place it?" Dino asked.

"No, I expect John's former employer must have."

"That's why it said so little," Viv commented

"I didn't know that he was at NYU Law when I was," Stone said, "until today. Lance accused me of being close to him in those years and not telling him."

"And Bill Eggers told me," Dino said, "that Collins was selling grass to the entire student body in those days."

"That was news to me, too," Stone said.

"It's also news to me," Vanessa said. "But it

explains why he seemed to have quite a lot of money when we married. A lot for someone so recently out of school, I mean. We bought furniture, we bought a car, and paid cash for everything."

"He must have been a saver," Dino said. "At least he wasn't smoking all his own product."

"He was abstemious in that regard," Vanessa said. "He hardly even drank."

"That's my cue," Dino said, "to tell you that I saw the Maine ME's report on him today, and he was stinking drunk when he was shot."

"I'm stunned to hear it," Vanessa said. "He was **afraid** of getting drunk. That's why he drank so little."

"Now that is something that two former homicide detectives would be interested in," Viv said. "I refer to Dino and Stone."

"That's interesting," Stone said, and Dino nodded.

"He would have had to have been forced at gunpoint to get drunk," Vanessa said.

"Maybe someone wanted information," Dino said, "something that the killer couldn't get out of him sober."

"People are forced to get drunk only in the movies," Viv said. "I've never known a single case of somebody being forced to drink."

"Neither have I," Stone said.

"Okay," Dino said, "neither have I. That makes it unanimous."

"Well," Vanessa said, "I'm glad we're all of one mind, but what does it mean?"

"It's a mystery," Stone said. "Maybe, if we're patient, information will come to light in the future that will explain everything."

"If you and I had followed that rule," Dino said, "we'd never have cleared a homicide."

"I was trying to give you a way out of explaining it," Stone said, "but having declined to accept my reasoning, go ahead and explain it to us."

"Maybe he got some bad news," Dino said. "Is there a bar on that ferry?"

"I've taken the ferry so rarely that I don't remember," Stone said. "I nearly always fly onto the island. But having a bar for people who are only going to be on board for twenty minutes doesn't seem like a working idea."

"Okay," Dino said. "You're a working stiff who toils away on the mainland every day, and you get on the ferry to go home, and there's a bar. You're going to turn down a drink?"

"All right, that's conceivable," Stone said, "but only just. The kind of people who live on the island are not working stiffs."

"And that kind of people don't like a drink at the end of the day?"

"If they do, they have it at home or, maybe, at the yacht club. We need a better story."

Nobody said anything.

11

"THAT WAS A NICE EVENING," Vanessa said, when they had returned to Stone's house for a nightcap. "Interesting people and conversation, even if it did seem to keep returning to John."

"I'm told that, at NYU, he was always called Jack by those who knew him."

"That was shortly before my time," she said. "He introduced himself as John, so I always called him that."

"Did you know a lot of people he knew at NYU?"

"No, I met him after he had gotten his law degree."

"How did you meet?"

"Through one of his old professors, a man named Samuel Bernard."

"Who was an active recruiter for the Agency over the years. Still is, for all I know. Is he how John was recruited?"

"It wouldn't surprise me to hear that. He was Bernard's great admirer."

"So is everyone who knows him. He made a pass at recruiting me, but I had fallen in love with police work and was no longer a prospect. So John was already an Agency officer when you met him?"

"Yes, he had just completed his training at the Farm, which he wouldn't talk about much. His first assignment was something at the UN— I never knew exactly what."

"Probably something to do with the Russians," Stone said, then he stopped himself with an idea.

"What?" she said. "You seem to have hit a roadblock."

"Nothing much," Stone said. "Anyway, I find you a more interesting subject than CIA recruitment."

She kissed him lightly, and Stone's index finger somehow came into contact with a nipple. "Now **that** was a good idea," she said.

He did it again, and this time with more intent. Everything was a little blurred, until they were naked in bed and had already achieved an orgasm.

"Now I feel more comfortable with you," Vanessa said.

"I should hope so. Is there anything else I can do that would make you even more comfortable?"

"As a matter of fact, there is," she said, pulling him down to her.

THE FOLLOWING MORNING, they had breakfast in bed and read the **Times** and watched **Morning Joe.** Stone's phone rang, and somehow he knew who it would be. Vanessa excused herself for the bathroom, and Stone picked up the phone. "Good morning, Lance."

"I hope I haven't caught you during an awkward moment," Lance said.

"It's all right. The awkward moment just went to the bathroom."

"Something occurred to me about your old and dear friend and classmate Collins," Lance said.

"Funny, something occurred to me about him, too, though he was neither an old nor dear friend, nor a classmate."

"You first," Lance said.

"Russians," Stone said. "Killing Collins sounds like something they would do, and pretty much the way they would do it."

"Funny you should mention that," Lance said. "The same thing occurred to me."

"Why are we singing the same song so early in the day?" Stone asked.

"Because we often think alike. Haven't you noticed that?"

What Stone had noticed was that if he had a good idea, Lance would adopt it as his own. "Not really," he said.

"Did your dinner with the widow produce anything new?"

"Only that she met him shortly after he had completed his training at the Farm, and that his first assignment was at the UN. It was the mention of the UN that made me think of the Russians."

"A logical leap," Lance said, "if you thought of the off-campus Russians instead of the officials."

"I did, but what would the Russians be doing in Maine?"

"Looking for Collins or, more likely, looking for you."

"That had not occurred to me, and it's an awful thought."

"They have long memories," Lance said. "I don't suppose their presence could have anything to do with your houseguest at the time?"

"That was, as you know, a top secret event."

"Except maybe over drinks at the Tarratine Yacht Club."

"Certainly the summer people would gossip, if they caught wind of her presence."

"Could Holly have been spotted on a boat with you, perhaps?"

"She always wore her hood up with sunglasses and no makeup, so probably not."

"Let's put that into the hopper and let it age for a bit. Let's not forget the Russians, though. I'll see what connections I can turn up."

Vanessa returned from the bathroom.

"You do that," Stone said, then hung up.

12

AFTER BREAKFAST AND the bathroom, Vanessa's thoughts lightly turned to more sex. Stone did what he could.

"Tell me," he said as they lay on their backs, taking deep breaths. "Did John Collins ever speak of Russians, with regard to his work at the UN?"

"Sort of, but mostly he seemed not to want to talk about anything to do with Russians. He had an aversion to them."

"Did he say why?"

"He once said that if the Russians knew he was CIA, they might want to harm him."

"Did he say why they would want to do that?"

"He said they hated everything to do with the CIA, especially the people who worked for them."

"But they didn't know he was CIA?"

"No, or they would have harmed him."

Stone thought that if he had enough sex with Vanessa, he might be able to figure out what John Collins was doing in Maine, and why he was killed.

"Did John ever say anything about Maine?"

"He said he had rented a little house there one summer before we met, and that we might like to go back sometime."

"And did you?"

"No, he never mentioned it again, and I forgot about it."

"Did he say where the house was?"

"In Lincolnville," she said.

"That's where the ferry to Islesboro runs from."

"I know. He said he liked to ride the ferry to Islesboro and drive around. It was very beautiful, but he couldn't afford a house there." She looked at her watch. "I have to go to work." She kissed him and left.

When Stone had showered, shaved, and dressed, he went down to his office and found Lance waiting for him, drinking coffee and eating a croissant.

"Good morning," Lance said. "You didn't tell me Helene made such wonderful croissants."

"I thought you had probably worked your way through the menu here," Stone said. "Are you just getting to croissants?"

"I need a full report on your activities of last evening," Lance said.

"Why do I think your request applies only to sex?"

"Well, it's very clear that that pump has to be primed before it produces anything, and you've just spent the night pumping."

"Did you ever send John Collins to Maine?"

"Why do you ask?"

"Because Vanessa says that he once rented a house for a summer in Lincolnville. I can't think of any reason why he should summer in Maine unless you dispatched him there."

"Interesting word, 'dispatched.' I mean, he was 'dispatched' there, wasn't he."

"Lance, you clearly know everything there is to know about John Collins, so why do you keep asking me to find out more about him?"

"Just filling in the gaps, old sport," Lance said.

"Why are there gaps in your knowledge of Collins?"

"Well, let's just say that, during his summer there, he was not reporting as regularly as I would have liked."

"I think we've pretty much scraped the bottom of that barrel, haven't we?"

"Have we? I'd like to know."

"Lance, why was Collins in Maine?"

Lance finished his coffee and set down the cup. "Because he wanted to kill somebody."

"Anybody in particular?"

"Oh, yes."

"Let me hazard a guess: a Russian?"

Lance thought about that for a moment. "Possibly."

"Why?"

"Retribution, I should imagine."

"Retribution for what?"

"For harming someone he was . . . fond of."

"A female person?"

"Yes."

"Was she CIA?"

"No, she worked at the UN for another country's service."

Before Stone could press him further, Lance was on his feet. "Must run," he said. "Can't waste that dose of caffeine." And he was gone.

13

Stone thought about it, and he realized that there was someone else who had seen John Collins on Islesboro. He made the call.

"Hahlo!"

"Seth, it's Stone."

"How you doin'?"

"Very well, thanks, and I hope you are."

"Yup."

"Seth, you remember the gentleman who spent the night in the garage?"

"Of course."

"Did you get a good look at him?"

"Of course. How could I miss him?"

"Right. Had you ever seen him before?"

"Yup."

"When and where?"

"I saw him in August. He was walking on the island. Noticed him because most of them from away drive their cars or golf carts."

"Walking where?"

"Just walking."

"I don't mean his destination. I mean, where on the island did you see him?"

"Two or three spots, I reckon."

"Where were they?"

"I saw him along the road from the ferry to the village, like maybe he had just gotten off the ferry. I saw him in the village, where he went into the store and bought an ice cream. I saw him, late in the day, walking back toward the ferry."

"How was he dressed?"

"Casual, like all them from away: khakis, a shirt; had a sweater thrown over his shoulders, like he expected it to get cooler. Good idea! It gets cooler up here."

"Was he alone?"

"Yup."

"How long was he in the store?"

"Twenty minutes, maybe. More than enough time to get himself an ice cream."

"Did you see him speak to anyone inside or outside the store?"

"When he come out, he gave a little wave to somebody behind him and said something. Couldn't make out what from the distance."

"Did he buy anything in the store except ice cream?"

Seth thought for a moment. "Yup. He bought a paper, maybe the New York one. Had it tucked under his arm."

"Which way did he go when he left the store?"

"Toward the ferry."

"Seth, is there a bar on the ferry, or liquor for sale?"

"Nope. You have to bring your own."

"Was he carrying anything? A bottle or a hip flask?"

"Nope to the bottle. His pants were kind of baggy, so he might have had room for a hip flask."

"Anything else you can remember about him?"

Seth went quiet for a minute.

"Seth?"

"Yup? Nope. Can't remember anything else."

"Thanks for your time, Seth."

"Yup." Seth hung up.

Stone ran the conversation again in his head and retained the pieces for further use.

Joan came in with some sheets of paper. "This was sent to you by Lance Cabot," she said.

It was the Maine ME's report on the Collins postmortem. Stone ran a finger down to "stomach contents"—**lobster, coleslaw, alcohol, colorless, likely vodka, eight to twelve drinks**—that spelled drunk.

So Collins had a lobster roll, widely available in the area, but vodka? Was liquor sold at the little market in Lincolnville? Very likely. But Collins was a nondrinker. What could have caused him to imbibe eight to twelve drinks? Or, perhaps, who? And where? On board the ferry? In a car? In a car on the way to the ferry?

Stone looked for the place on the form for cuts and bruises. One large bruise, recent, base of the skull. He would have been unconscious for a while afterward. That would account for how they got him into a car. Maybe how they had gotten the vodka into him.

Stone checked the photographs of the corpse. Fingernails intact and clean. He hadn't tried to scratch or claw anybody. Left-hand knuckles bruised. A straight left to somebody's nose, maybe. Right knuckles unbruised. A right to the belly or solar plexus? Bruises on both arms, just above the elbows. Somebody pinned his arms back? Maybe while pouring the vodka into him? None of this would count in a court of law, but it gave him a picture, albeit a fuzzy one.

He called Vanessa Morgan.

"Hi, there."

"Hi. Did the Agency send you or give you a package or a bag of the contents of John's pockets?"

"Yes, they did."

"Could you bring it with you to dinner tonight?"

"Okay."

"Six-thirty here?"

"Sure."

"See you then." They both hung up.

14

Vanessa appeared on time and Stone led her to his study, where he exchanged a drink for a ziplock plastic bag. "Do you mind if I look through these things now?" he asked her.

"Go right ahead."

Stone emptied the bag onto the coffee table. "Have you been through this?" he asked her.

"Nope, they look just like the stuff he laid on the dresser top every night he was home."

Stone poked through the contents. "There should be a wallet with his CIA ID," he said.

"The guy who delivered the bag said they never found it."

"Right." Stone found a tiny cardholder with John's Agency business cards; he kept one. There was a thick wallet, and Stone counted eight hundred and ten dollars. He handed it to Vanessa. "Here, go spend that."

"Consider it done," she said, dropping it into her handbag.

"Did he often carry that much cash?"

"It's not unusual, for him."

Stone took an assortment of credit cards from the wallet and spread them on the table: Amex, Visa, ATM card, and one that was blank except for a ten-digit number.

"That blank card is for a bank, isn't it?" Vanessa asked.

"Could be. Did John do any banking outside the country?"

"Like where?"

"Like Macao, the Cayman Islands, Malta, Cyprus?"

"We went to the Caymans once. St. George's, for three days."

"Did John ever leave you alone when you were there? A couple of hours, maybe?"

"Yes, we were lying on a beach, and I fell asleep. When I woke up, he was gone, and he didn't come back for another hour or more. I asked him where he'd been, and he said, 'Just taking a stroll.'"

"When you went to the beach, did he take any sort of luggage with him?"

"He took a canvas duffel with his towel and

sunglasses in it, that sort of thing. He was carrying it when he came back, but it looked emptier."

Stone went through the other detritus in the
wallet, and it was just that. Stone handed her
the numbered card. "When John used the ATM
card, do you know what the PIN was?"

"Yes, it was 5350. Mine, too. That was the
house number of a place we lived right after we
got married."

"Did he use any other PINs?"

"No, just that one. Me, too."

"Tell you what: tomorrow, find a bank with
an ATM, put the blank card into it, and try
to withdraw five hundred dollars, using your
regular PIN."

"Do you think it will cough it up?"

"Maybe, and maybe it will cough up a lot
more. Are you good with computers?"

"Pretty good."

"Tomorrow, go online, using that ten-digit
number and 'Cayman Islands,' and do a Google
search. If you find anything to do with a bank,
see if you can get into their website, using your
PIN. You might find it a pleasant experience."

"Okay."

They had dinner.

"Do you think the blank bank account might
really have any money in it?"

"Bank accounts are all alike. They have in them

what somebody has deposited, less what someone has taken out. Can you remember a time when John made a large cash purchase?"

"Yes, he bought me a Mercedes convertible—not a new one, but several years old—and he wrote a check for sixty-five thousand dollars to pay for it. The check was a different color than our usual checkbook, and now that I think of it, the name St. George's was printed on it. I asked him about it, and he told me, laughing, to mind my own business."

"Did John have a will?"

"We both do—did."

"Have you read it yet?"

"No, we just left everything to each other."

"Dig it out tomorrow and see exactly what it says."

"All right."

After dinner, it didn't take long for them to get into bed.

THE FOLLOWING MORNING, Stone was at his desk when the phone rang. "Hello?"

"Vanessa Morgan on one."

Stone pressed the button. "Good morning, did you get to work on time?"

"I was a couple of minutes late. I had to stop at an ATM."

"Did it work?"

"It did, and now I have five hundred dollars I hadn't expected to have."

"Well, you have eight hundred from John's wallet, too."

"Can anybody hear us on this line?"

"No, it's entirely private, and I have my phones swept regularly for bugs."

Her voice became more confidential. "I got on my computer when I came to work, and I found a bank account associated with the blank card."

"I rather thought you might. Is there anything in it?"

"Does this call come under attorney-client privilege?"

"First you have to hire me as your attorney."

"Okay, you're hired, starting now."

"Then you're covered."

"The account balance is a million six hundred thousand dollars."

"Wow."

"What does this mean?"

"It means you're a million six richer than you were yesterday. Can you print out a statement?"

"There's a button for that."

"E-mail me a copy of the statement."

"Okay. I have a confidential question."

"Shoot."

"Is the money in this account tax-free?"

"Generally speaking, any income you receive is taxable, unless it's deductible."

"Well, I know that, but is my new million six tax-free? I mean, if I don't pay taxes on it, will anybody know?"

"I'm sorry, I didn't hear that."

"I said, Will anybody know, if I don't pay taxes on it?"

"We must have a bad line. I can't hear a word you're saying."

"I get it."

"I didn't hear that, either. Bye-bye." He hung up, and buzzed Joan.

"Yes, sir?"

"Scan and send a standard representation memo and a bill for a hundred dollars to Vanessa Morgan."

15

Stone called a private line at the Agency.
"Lance Cabot."

"Lance, it's Stone."

"What can I do for you, Stone? Busy morning."

"Have you read the Maine medical examiner's report on the autopsy of John Collins?"

"It's right here on my desk."

"You should read it. It tells quite a story."

"Save me some time and tell me the story."

"John Collins, it appears, was knocked unconscious and had vodka poured down his throat, then he was taken aboard the Islesboro ferry, probably in a car or van, shot twice in the head and left there for dead, which he was. He was probably ferried from the island to Lincolnville. The ferry got hit by a big wind and was blown sideways in the channel, so in the effort to straighten it out and get it moored in Lincolnville, nobody came across the dead body for quite some time."

"And you know all this, how?"

"By reading the autopsy report." Stone hung up.

Half an hour later, Joan buzzed him. "Lance Cabot on one."

"Yes, Lance."

"I've read the report and had a chat with the ME up there, and after some prodding he confirmed your view of his report."

"Well, that makes my day," Stone replied.

"Don't be sarcastic, Stone. It doesn't suit you."

"I was expressing irony, not sarcasm."

"What do you want me to do about this?"

"I don't know, what do you usually do when an officer under your command is kidnapped and murdered on home soil?"

"Irony again?"

"That was sarcasm, founded on your apparent indifference to the loss of an officer."

"I am not indifferent to our loss."

"Good. I'll look forward to the results of your investigation."

"I will appoint an ad hoc commission to investigate the matter."

"On which I will not serve," Stone said. "I've read our contract and it does not require or permit me to run internal investigations."

"I don't like you throwing your contract up to me every time we disagree."

"I'm a lawyer. Contracts are what I do. And this is the first time I've mentioned my contract when we've disagreed."

"And don't do it again."

"I'll reserve the right to do it anytime we disagree," Stone said.

"Will you assent to advising the ad hoc committee?"

"When they're done, I'll read their report and make any comments about the results that I feel are pertinent."

"I don't think I'll want you to do that," Lance said.

"Are you afraid I'll disagree with them?"

"You almost certainly will."

"Then you think they'll lie in their report?"

"I'm sure they'll do the right thing."

"And who gets to determine what's right?"

"I do," Lance said, then hung up.

Stone buzzed Joan.

"Yes, sir?"

"Please bring me a copy of my contract with the CIA."

16

Stone and Dino were having dinner at Clarke's when Lance entered the dining room and sat down at their table.

"Would you like to join us, Lance?" Stone asked.

"Thank you, I already have," Lance replied, waving at a passing waiter and ordering a steak. "Would you like something?" Lance asked Stone.

"Thank you, we've already ordered."

"I want to talk to you about the John Collins matter."

"Is it all right if Dino listens in?"

"Dino has the same clearances as you," Lance said.

"Granted, but I'm not sure he has the same tolerance for unadulterated horseshit," Stone replied.

"Goddamn it, Stone," Lance said, unusually

profane, "you're meddling in something that's not your business!"

"Oh, really? A man, an employee of the federal government, leaves the island of my summer home, and boards or is dragged forcibly onto the local ferry, where he is beaten by likely two, probably three, men and forced to drink an entire bottle of vodka, then knocked unconscious and shot twice in the head. His body is abandoned there, later to be brought to and stored in my garage. Subsequently, I am able to discover, by the simple device of reading, that he is carrying a large sum of cash and has a seven-figure balance in an offshore bank and likely connections to the Russian mob. Please tell me how this is not **everybody's** business."

"Yeah," Dino said. "I want to hear this."

The waiter came and set Lance's steak before him.

"Hey!" Dino yelled. "We ordered half an hour ago! Where are **our** steaks?"

"We're felling an ox now," the waiter shouted back over his shoulder, then disappeared into the kitchen.

"He knows I'm in a hurry," Lance said, sawing a chunk off his steak.

"Answer my question," Stone said to Lance.

"Yeah," Dino echoed. "Why isn't it **everybody's** business?"

Lance poured himself a glass of wine. "Because

I decide whose business it is, and I have decided that it is not yours."

"Then why did you ask me to chair an investigation into the circumstances of his death?"

"I didn't ask you to chair, just advise," Lance said, making a large portion of a baked potato disappear. "And I realize that was a mistake because you chose that moment to be unhelpful."

"You chose the moment. And you didn't want the matter investigated, just buried."

"Are you now, belatedly, offering to chair the investigation?"

"No. Once again, I am declining to be associated with a CIA cover-up."

"You make it sound as if my province is cover-ups," Lance said hotly.

"It is when you want to cover up something, and you clearly want the Collins matter covered up. Besides, I've already given you a full explanation of what happened to Collins. I just want to know why."

"What is your reason?"

"Because Collins's widow is my client, and **she** wants to know."

"So you want to haul an innocent woman into this, just to satisfy your own curiosity?"

"That's a good enough reason, though not the only one."

"Children, children," Dino sang out. "Please!

You're disturbing the other diners. Now **they** want to know what's going on!"

"Tell them to go fuck themselves," Lance said, but he did lower his voice.

"Ladies and gentlemen," Dino announced to the room, "the director . . ."

Lance stabbed at Dino's hand with a fork, barely missing, but it had the effect of interrupting his announcement.

"Dino," Lance said, "you came within an ace of violating federal law by divulging classified information. If I hadn't stopped you, you would now be on your way to a federal detention center."

"So now you're threating the poor, innocent police commissioner with arrest and imprisonment," Stone said.

"Would you like me to include you?" Lance asked.

The maître d' strolled over. "Gentlemen, gentlemen," he said soothingly. "If you keep this up, Mr. Cabot is going to have to arrest the whole dining room, and that would be bad for business. Cool it, please!"

Lance carved a chunk of steak. Stone stabbed it and stuffed it into his mouth. "I'm starved," he explained, then stood up. "I will seek out dining companions elsewhere," he said, and stalked out of the dining room.

"His check is yours," Dino said.

17

THE FOLLOWING MORNING, Stone called Ed Rawls at his home on Islesboro.

"Yes?"

"It's Stone, Ed. How are you?"

"I'm all right. I take it you're not, or you wouldn't be calling me."

"I'm trying to get to the bottom of this Collins thing," Stone said, "and I keep running up against Lance Cabot."

"And that surprises you?"

"It does. Have you seen the Maine ME's report?"

"No."

Stone told him what it contained and why he thought the things he did.

"That's all logical, I guess. What doesn't Lance like about logical?"

"That's what I can't figure out. He sat down with Dino and me at Clarke's last evening and harangued us for half an hour."

"On what subject?"

"That we should keep our noses out of the Collins affair. What I can't figure out is why Lance doesn't want to know what happened to the man."

"Well, obviously, Lance has a proprietary interest in Collins."

"As you say, obviously, but why doesn't he want to know more?"

"Maybe he already knows more, but he doesn't want you and Dino to."

"I can't figure out why."

"Look, Lance has a lot more stuff crossing his desk than just Collins, and maybe some of it relates. For instance, why did he place an officer in the Penobscot Bay area? That's a bit far afield, even for Lance."

"I know. And what are Russians doing up there? Have you seen anything that says 'Russians' to you?"

"You can bet your ass that if there are Russians up here, they've taken great pains to appear not to be."

"Okay, I'll buy that."

"And maybe, by sitting at P. J. Clarke's and shouting at Lance about it, you're causing an atmospheric disturbance."

18

STONE WAS WONDERING what he was going to do for dinner, when he got a call explaining it to him.

"Hi, it's Vanessa. Let's have dinner."

"What a good idea!"

"Let's try the new restaurant at the Carlyle," she suggested.

"You're just full of good ideas."

"I'll book, and I'll meet you there at seven."

"Done." He hung up, his spirits lightened.

THE PLACE HAD been redone, and it was handsome—new décor and lots of flowers. They nestled into a corner table. Their drink order came, and they raised their glasses. "Do you want to hear the latest about John Collins?"

Before he could stop himself, he said, "Sure."

"He's not dead."

Stone got his swallow down before he checked her face for signs that she was kidding. "No kidding?"

"No kidding. We talked on the phone for half an hour this afternoon. In fact, he suggested you and I have dinner together, and where."

Stone surveyed the room.

"He's not here," she said. "I already checked."

"So you're not a widow anymore?"

"Nope."

"I liked you as a widow."

"Frankly, so did I, but I'm glad he's all right. He's recovering well from the gunshot wounds and the beating he took. He said they forced a bottle of vodka down his throat, but he threw up some of it."

"Is there a punch line in here somewhere?" Stone asked.

"That's what I was waiting for on the phone call, but it was full of little references that only he and I would have understood. It couldn't have been faked."

"How did he feel about being cremated and scattered at sea?"

"He thanked me for following his wishes."

"Did he give you any sort of explanation or account of what happened?"

"He said I'd have to wait awhile, but that he would fully explain at a later date."

"Did he say where he's been since we last saw him?"

"In treatment and recovery."

"Where?"

"He couldn't say. I guess he's afraid of it happening again."

"Did he say who the guy was who spent a night in my garage in Maine?"

"No, and he wasn't allowed to say what he was doing in Maine, either."

"Does Lance Cabot know about this?"

"He said that Lance knows just about everything."

"'Just about'? He's holding back something?"

"John always holds back. He tells me only what he wants me to know. He says it is for my protection."

"The next time he calls, ask him if he'll come over for a drink. I'd like to have a chat with him."

"Funny, he suggested that he do that, when he's better."

"He knows who I am?"

"He didn't at the time, but he does now."

"You told him all about me, huh?"

"I did, and he was happy for me."

"Well, as long as he's happy, I guess it doesn't matter if he's dead."

"You don't seem to be taking the news very seriously, Stone."

"Well, you sort of sprang it on me. I must say, I wasn't expecting to hear it."

"Life's like that," she said. "You think you know everything, and suddenly it jumps up and bites you in the ass."

"You're a philosopher, Vanessa. Are there any Greeks on your family tree?"

She laughed, then they ordered another drink and perused the menu.

LATER, AFTER THEY had made love, Stone started to ask a question, but Vanessa stopped him. "No more questions," she said. "I've told you all I'm allowed to tell you."

"Who's doing the allowing?"

"I said, no more questions. If you have enough energy to ask me questions, use it to fuck me again."

"As I said earlier, you're just full of good ideas." He took her advice.

19

VANESSA INSISTED ON sleeping in her own bed, and just after Stone had seen her off, Lance called. "Good evening."

"It's not evening, Lance. It's very early in the morning."

"Oh. Sorry about that. I have important news."

"I've already heard it," Stone said.

"That's impossible."

"No, it's not, Lance. I got it from the horse's mouth."

"I assure you, **I am** the horse's mouth."

"All right, you first," Stone said.

"No, you first."

"All right, the Japanese have just bombed Pearl Harbor."

"Be serious."

"We lost six battleships. That's not serious?"

"I order you to shut up and listen," Lance said.

"I'm listening."

Lance was silent for a moment. "Now I can't remember what I was going to tell you."

"Was it that John Collins is still alive?"

"It most certainly was not."

"I just thought I'd take a stab."

"I'll call you back when I can remember why I called."

"Could you make it after seven AM?" Stone asked. "Then I can drown you out with the TV news." He hung up, and so did Lance.

A moment later, the phone rang again. "I forgot to tell you something," Vanessa said. "Don't tell Lance Cabot that John is still alive."

"I'm afraid I've already told him, but he didn't believe me."

"That's good. Let's keep it that way until tomorrow afternoon. John's request. He wants to tell Lance himself."

"All right," Stone said. "Good night." He hung up.

Stone was nodding off when the phone rang again.

"Hello."

"It's Lance. I've just received the most preposterous note."

"Don't tell me, it was from John Collins, saying he was still alive."

"**What?** How could you possibly know that?"

"I gave you that news earlier this evening."

"Yes, but of course I didn't believe you."

"Did you believe the guy who sent you the note?"

"He told me some things that only he and I could know, so I believe him."

"Okay, can I go back to sleep now?"

"Yes, I suppose so."

"If you think of anything else, don't call me," Stone said. He tried to hang up before Lance did, but he wasn't fast enough.

The phone rang again, but Stone pulled a pillow over his head and did his best to ignore it. Eventually, it stopped ringing.

STONE HAD JUST gotten his breakfast off the dumbwaiter when the phone rang again.

"Is this Lance Cabot or John Collins?" Stone asked.

"That wasn't funny," Lance said.

"I thought it was logical, in the circumstances."

"I remembered why I called you the first time last night."

"Shoot."

"The first meeting of the commission to investigate the death of John Collins is at three this afternoon, and it will be conducted online by your cochair, Hugh English."

"I have two reasons for declining to accept that news," Stone said. "One, I will have nothing to do with Hugh English, who is a self-righteous son of a bitch. In fact, I thought you had already ejected him from your service. Two, I assume that John Collins is not dead. That's from the horse's mouth."

"Hugh has agreed to stay on for a few months to wrap up the commission."

"**Months**? For a man who's not dead yet?"

"It must be thorough."

"Well, they will only have to call one witness: Mr. Collins. That should be thorough enough."

"You're assuming that Collins is still alive."

"I am. I got it from an unimpeachable source." He hung up and buzzed Joan.

"Yes, sir?"

"Hold all my calls, especially any from Lance Cabot or Hugh English."

"Okay, who's Hugh English?"

"That's need-to-know information." He hung up.

20

WHEN STONE GOT to his desk he found a phone message from Sergeant Young of the Maine State Police. He called back.

"Sergeant Young."

"Good morning. It's Stone Barrington, returning your call."

"Oh, yes, Stone, thank you for calling."

"What's up?"

"I've had reports that someone calling himself John Collins has been seen on Islesboro."

"Yes, Mr. Collins seems pretty active for a dead man," Stone replied.

"I thought that, too. Have you heard anything about this?"

"I've heard from two people who ought to

know that they've received phone calls from him and were convinced that the caller was real."

"Real what?"

"Real alive."

"And the real John Collins?"

"Yes."

"Have you spoken to this man?"

"No, but if he should call me, I have no means of contradicting him. We never met, until he was dead."

"Was one of these persons you talked to Lance Cabot?"

"I'm afraid I can't confirm or deny that, but the other person was Collins's widow, so to speak."

"And she was convinced he was the real McCoy?"

"No, just the real John Collins. Both the people who heard from him say that he had information known only to the person who called."

"I see," Young said, though he clearly did not.

"Have you heard from someone claiming to be Collins?" Stone asked.

"Not yet, but the way things are going, I wouldn't be surprised if I did."

"If it's any help, his description of his . . . Well, of the attack on him, matched the bruises on your ME's report. How many people, to your knowledge, have seen the ME's report?"

"I don't know," Young said. "Half a dozen had cause to see it, I suppose, but after it was filed, it became a public record, and anyone could have seen it."

"You might ask the person in charge of records how many people have asked for it, and their names."

"Mmmm, yes." Young didn't sound very interested in knowing.

"Let's put it this way: Who would have something to gain by reading the report?"

"How about whoever is pretending to be John Collins?"

"I'll buy that, but tell me: Why is that person so good at pretending to be Collins that he is able to fool his boss and his wife?"

"I think I'm just going to have to accept that it's the real Collins, until somebody proves me wrong."

"I think that's a sensible approach to the problem," Stone said. "If he contacts you, try to arrange a meeting and photograph him and/or get his fingerprints on something."

"I don't think I could recognize him if I met him," Young said. "After all, the only time I've seen him was after he was dead."

"Do you have a record of any of his IDs?"

"No, they were either taken by the Agency or missing."

"Do you have any reason to believe that Collins has committed a crime in your jurisdiction?"

"I don't know. I'm not sure that pretending to be dead is a crime in Maine."

"It would be if it was for a nefarious purpose," Stone said.

"Nefarious. I like that word."

"Yes, it covers a multitude of sins, doesn't it."

"I wonder if Collins had any money; somebody might want that."

"He had some pay and a pension coming from the Agency." Stone didn't mention the million six in the Cayman bank account. After all, that was confidential information.

"You wouldn't think a man would pretend to be dead in order to collect his own pension, would you?"

"I wouldn't, but who knows?"

"Stone, will you call if you get any other information I can use?"

"Information that he's dead or not dead?"

"Either. I don't really care which." Young hung up.

21

THE FOLLOWING MORNING Stone got a call from Vanessa.

"Stone, if John is to remain legally dead, do I need an accountant?"

"I was under the impression that you already had one. But I'll be happy to recommend someone. You'll need an accountant to close out the estate and file a final tax return. Call Bertrand James." He gave her the number. "He'll tell you what has to be done. One thing he could do for you is to write, on your behalf, to all of John's creditors and instruct them to send final bills, then close his accounts. Do you have a death certificate?"

"Yes."

"Then give that to Bert and he can send copies to the creditors. By the way, you'll have to decide what you're going to do about the Cayman account. If you're going to declare it, tell Bert."

"And if not, don't?"

"Sorry, I couldn't hear that. Bye."

"I'll call him right now." She hung up.

Dino called. "You heard anything from the late John Collins?"

"Nope, not a word. Vanessa is instructing an accountant now on closing the estate."

"That's always fun."

"It is, if you discover unexpected riches; it's not, if you discover unexpected debts."

"Dinner tonight?"

"Sure. Clarke's at seven?"

"Done." They both hung up.

LATE IN THE afternoon, Sergeant Young of the Maine State Police called.

"Good afternoon," Stone said.

"I've thought a lot about our conversation, and I've decided that the Collins case will be a lot less trouble if I assume he's alive."

"If you say so. By the way, who was the man who was shot on the ferry?"

"The murder victim?"

"Right. If Collins is alive, who's the victim?"

"I guess I'll have to investigate that."

"Where are you going to start? I mean, you don't have the corpse, so you can't pull prints or a DNA sample. Do you still have his clothes?"

"I guess those would be with the ME."

"He might have printed the corpse, too, or kept a tissue sample for DNA. I should think that would be standard practice."

"I'll give him a call now," Young said, then hung up.

STONE WAS ON his first drink at the bar when his phone rang. "Hello?"

"Mr. Barrington?"

"Yes?"

"This is John Collins, how are you?"

"Ah, the mysterious Mr. Collins! A better question to ask might be: How are you? You certainly don't sound dead."

Collins chuckled. "I'm relieved to hear that."

"Where are you?" Stone asked. "Can you join me for dinner at P. J. Clarke's?"

"I'm in the city, but I have another commitment. Vanessa suggested we meet, though. How about tomorrow night?"

"Fine. Do you know Patroon?"

"Yes."

"Let's meet there at seven o'clock. I'll book."

"See you then," Collins said, then hung up before Stone could ask any further questions.

Dino pulled up a stool, and the bartender set a Scotch before him. "Sorry I'm late."

"If you had been here a few minutes earlier, you could have witnessed a phone conversation between the spirit of John Collins and me."

"He called?"

"Yes, and we have a dinner date tomorrow evening at Patroon. Would you like to join us?"

"You mean you want a witness."

"Well, yes. And a fingerprint and a DNA sample."

"If you get all that and have me as a witness, then the mystery ends?"

"Unless he turns out not to be John Collins."

"Then a new mystery begins," Dino said. "I love a mystery."

22

WHEN STONE GOT home he walked into the house and heard someone clearing his throat. He went to the study and found Lance Cabot sitting on the sofa before a fire, a drink in his hand.

"All cozy, are we?"

"Come in, Stone."

"Thank you so much," Stone replied. He poured himself a brandy. "Something more for you?"

"I'm fine. Have a seat."

"Thank you." Stone sank into the other end of the sofa and took a sip of brandy. "You seem pensive, Lance. What's going on?"

"I may have to kill John Collins."

"Again? Wasn't once enough?"

"Apparently not."

Stone sat quietly and waited for Lance to explain.

"If you hear from him, you have to tell me."

"Why?"

"Because if I'm going to kill him, I have to find him, and you, perhaps, might help."

"Why do you think I would become involved in a murder?"

"If he's already dead, it wouldn't be murder, would it?"

"If he's alive, it would be."

"Have you heard from him?"

"Why would he get in touch with me?"

"He may be jealous. I mean, you are fucking his wife."

"His widow. And any fucking we may have done was conducted on that basis."

"I don't think he sees it that way."

"Well, I wouldn't know about how he sees things."

"Will you let me know if he contacts you?"

"I don't think I will," Stone said. "What you've told me could make me complicit in a murder."

"Oh, don't come over all legal on me."

"It's what I do. I have to live as I advise my clients. Tell me, what has he done to deserve being murdered?"

"He has disappointed me."

"Oh, that. Surely others who have disappointed you have not been punished by death."

"Not many."

Stone didn't want to know about that.

"He's getting money from somewhere."

"Everybody has to eat."

"I've had a watch on his accounts, so it can't be coming from those. Have you given him money?"

"He hasn't gotten a cent from me."

"Vanessa may have found some way to get it to him."

"She hasn't confided in me."

"It's hard to run down a man who doesn't appear to need money."

"I haven't had any experience with that."

"Maybe he has an offshore account that I don't know about."

Stone sighed and had another sip of brandy.

"Does he?" Lance asked.

"If you don't know that, why would I?"

"Why do you keep giving me evasive answers?"

"I'm just trying to stay logical. Your assumption seems to be that I know all about Collins, but I don't. You know a great deal about him, so why are you asking me these things?"

"Because I think that if you knew something that I should know, you wouldn't tell me."

Stone polished off his brandy. "This is becoming tiresome, Lance, so I'm going to bed. You know where the guest rooms are, so pick one." He stood up. "Good night."

Lance didn't respond, so Stone walked out of

the room and went upstairs. As he walked into his bedroom a light came on in the security panel, then it went out. Apparently, Lance had opened and closed the front door. Stone armed the system and got into bed. The phone rang.

"Hello?"

"It's Vanessa. How are you?"

"Sleepy. I was just going to bed."

"I wish I were there with you."

"Then neither of us would get any sleep."

"John called me again tonight."

"And what did he have to say?"

"Nothing of any substance. He wants to meet you."

"Why?"

Silence.

"I have to go to sleep now. Is there anything else that can't wait until tomorrow?"

"I guess not."

"Good night, then." He hung up and was soon asleep.

23

STONE ARRIVED AT Patroon before dinner and was shown to their usual table. A martini was set down across the table for him.

"For your guest," the waiter said. "Your usual?"

"Yes, please."

Stone's cell phone rang. "Yes?"

"It's Jack Collins."

"Good evening. Your martini awaits you."

"It's my understanding that you've invited another guest. Who is he?"

"His name is Dino Bacchetti."

"The police commissioner of New York?"

"That is correct. Dino and I were partners when we were police detectives."

"I'm not sure I'm comfortable with this."

"Why? Have you committed a crime in New York?"

"Well, no."

"Then what's the problem?"

Silence for a moment. "You want a witness," Collins said.

"I do. You may bring one, too, if you like."

"Who would I bring?"

"Anyone you like. Anyone you trust."

"There are very few of those."

"Then don't bring one," Stone said. "Your martini is getting warm."

A man slid into the seat across from him, raised his glass, and sipped his martini.

"You're wearing a disguise," Stone said. "Gray wig, eyebrows, and moustache. Who are you hiding from?"

"From those who might wish to harm me."

"Who are they?"

"I have my suspicions, but I can't prove it yet."

"Who tried to kill you?"

"Russian mobsters, I believe."

"And whom did they kill instead?"

"Someone I sent to a meeting on my behalf."

"Was he Agency?"

"You know enough about them to know that I can't answer that."

"You could if the answer was no. Since it's not, he was. How did you choose him for the task?"

"I trusted him, and he was willing."

"Did he impersonate you?"

"Yes."

"You must feel bad about what happened to him."

"I do, and I expect to exact revenge, at some point."

"Where were you when he was shot?"

"Observing."

"And where was he?"

"On the ferry, at their request."

"Given the weather, it would have been very difficult for you to observe from ashore."

"You have a point."

"Why did the Russians want you dead?"

"Because I know their plans."

"What are their plans?"

"I think it's best that you don't have that information just yet."

"Why not?"

"Because then they would want you dead, too."

"Why haven't they tried again?"

"Because they don't know what I look like."

"Thus, your disguise?"

"You're very quick. The disguise protects you, too."

"Ah."

Dino arrived and was seated before Collins could bolt. Stone introduced the two men.

"Think of Dino as part of your disguise," Stone said.

"How so?"

"Because they wouldn't expect you to be dining with the police commissioner."

Collins laughed. "Point taken."

"Would you like to order?"

"Thank you, I'll have the Dover sole."

"And a Caesar salad? Very good here."

"Thank you, yes."

They ordered.

"Another martini?" Stone asked.

"No, I think I'd better keep my wits about me."

"I assume you've checked the exits and plotted an escape route."

Collins smiled. "Why do you think that?"

"Because that's what they taught you at the Farm."

"Quite right."

"Now, Jack, why did you request this meeting?"

"Because I wanted to see if you are good enough for my wife to be sleeping with."

"May I remind you that when we met, she and I both thought her a widow."

"I suppose, for all practical purposes, she is."

"Then you're not planning a resurrection as John Collins?"

"I think not."

"By the way, you should know that you no longer have access to the Cayman bank account."

Collins displayed a slight alarm. "Why not?"

"Because Vanessa changed the account number and password—at my suggestion."

"Why did you suggest it?"

"Because you removed four hundred fifty thousand dollars at a time when we both thought you dead."

"That's inconvenient."

"I'm sure Vanessa will give you the new codes, if you ask for them."

"Do you have them?"

"It's not my account. By the way, she's closing whatever other accounts you may have."

"Why?"

"Because a dead person can't have such accounts."

"I hadn't counted on that."

"Then you should have trusted her sooner than you did. I'll leave the two of you to sort that out."

Stefan, the headwaiter, turned up tableside to do his magic with the Caesar salad. They turned their attention to him.

24

THEY CHATTED AMIABLY through dinner, and Stone rather liked the man. He tried to imagine him without the disguise and failed.

"Have you spoken to Lance recently?" Stone asked.

"Not since my death, though I sent him a message that he would know was authentic."

"You might give him a call. He could smooth your way into a new identity."

"I don't feel that I need one."

"You'll just go on wearing the wig, then?"

"I don't feel I'll need that, either."

"You think you'll be done with the Russians soon, then?"

"Soon enough."

"I've had some experience with them," Stone said, "and I found them to be unreasonably tenacious."

"And where did you encounter them? Or them, you?"

"In Los Angeles, New York, and Paris."

"There must be rather a lot of them," Collins said.

"They make it seem so. If you think you might need Lance, you should contact him sooner rather than later. He likes being needed, and he prefers information from the source rather than from rumor."

"I suppose you've had some experience with Lance, then."

"A good deal. When he's in New York I find him in my home two or three times a week, and at my table whenever he's hungry."

"What is it about you that attracts him, do you think?"

"He likes my lifestyle better than his own."

"I may have to go to ground for a while."

"I understand you like Islesboro?"

"I do, very much."

"I have a house there, if you want to stay out of sight for a while. After Labor Day, the island is practically deserted."

"That's a kind offer, and I may accept it."

"Call me before you leave, so I can let the care-takers know you're coming."

"How many are there?"

"Only a couple, Seth and Mary Hotchkiss. She's a fine cook. You won't lose any weight up there."

"It sounds more and more attractive."

"If you intend to roam the island, use your disguise and stay out of the Dark Harbor store. The owner, Jimmy, substitutes for radio, television, and the newspaper, and he publishes hourly. If you need supplies, Seth will get them for you, and the daily papers, too."

"Good to know."

"Does the name Ed Rawls mean anything to you?"

"I met him once, at Langley. He wouldn't remember. I know his story."

"He'll know your story, too, and he lives on the island just about year round. You'll need an introduction before you go calling on him; he's well-armed, testy, and a crack shot. Call me before you seek him out."

"I'll do that."

"Do you know anyone who has a light aircraft?"

"Yes, I do. An elderly Beech Bonanza, the V-tail."

"Has it had the modification to the empennage that keeps it from falling off in turbulence?"

"It has."

"Then that's the best way onto the island. The strip is 2,450 feet. Your airplane shouldn't find it a problem."

"I've seen it when on foot."

"Seth will meet you there and transport you and your luggage to the house. Do you know anything about the history of the place?"

"I know it was built by your cousin Dick Stone."

"And to Agency standards. It will repel small-arms fire."

"Is there a boat?"

"There are two, but the sailing yacht is stored ashore until spring. There's a Hinckley Picnic Boat at my dock. Seth has the keys. There are two cars, a 1938 Ford woodie station wagon and a 1954 MG TF 1500, both readily identifiable as belonging to me. Don't use them if that concerns you."

"Got it."

"If you're likely to need a quick escape, refuel at Rockland before you land. There's no fuel on the island."

"Right."

"One last thing: arm the security system whenever you're inside. Seth will show you how. There are weapons in a hidden office under the stairs, and a computer link to Langley."

Jack nodded. "I'm familiar."

"Oh, there's one gap in the security. The back porch can be seen readily from the harbor, so a good shot on a boat could nail you, even in the living room. Draw the curtains at dusk."

"I'd like to go up there the day after tomorrow, from the airport at Caldwell, New Jersey."

Stone wrote some things down in his note-book, tore out the page, and gave it to Collins. "Phone numbers. I'll let the couple and Rawls know you're coming."

"Thanks."

"If you're looking to repair relationships, Vanessa would like it there. This time of the year, there are no available women present."

Collins nodded. "Excuse me. I need the men's room." He left the table.

Five minutes later, the owner, Ken Aretsky, came over. "Your guest had to leave. The check has been paid."

"What a good guest," Dino said.

"You were very quiet," Stone pointed out.

"Sometimes you learn more by listening. You should try it."

"And what did you learn about Jack Collins?"

"That he's a very careful man," Dino replied.

25

STONE WAS AT his desk the following morning when Joan buzzed him.

"Lance, on one."

"Good morning, Lance."

"How was your dinner meeting last evening?" Lance drawled.

"Not unpleasant."

"Did you like him?"

"I didn't dislike him."

"Where is he now?"

"He gave me no clue to his current whereabouts. He's a careful man."

"If a bit distrustful."

"I had the impression that he was probably a good judge of whom to mistrust."

"Did you?"

"Does he trust you, Lance?"

"I haven't had an opportunity to ask him."

"Do you have knowledge of his quarrels with the Russians?"

"I've picked up tidbits."

"Anything you'd like to share?"

"He distrusts them."

"Well, they keep trying to kill him. That would do it for most people. Was he a good officer when he was still on board?"

"Better than average."

"Then he knows how to stay alive."

"What did you two talk about?"

"The Russians, mostly. He passed on dessert and left early."

"An old trick from the Farm."

"I guessed."

"Did you offer him succor?"

"He seemed very self-sufficient."

"My advice to you is don't get too fond of him."

"Is he going somewhere?"

"Wherever he likes, I suspect."

"How do you rate his chances against the Russians?"

"He has an edge, since they don't know how to find him."

"How do you know they don't?"

"Because they haven't. I'm sure we'll hear about it if they do."

"Would he be welcome at home?"

"Possibly. That would have to be negotiated."

"Would you like him to know that, should I hear from him again?"

"You can pass it along, if you like."

"I will, if I do."

"Don't weigh too heavily on his side."

"I remain neutral. I'm happy to be an honest broker, should you need one."

"At your usual thousand dollars an hour?"

"Good help doesn't come cheap, Lance. You can probably find an honest broker for two hundred an hour, but he won't be honest, and he won't be a broker."

"Tell me about it. Oh, something you can pass on, should you hear from him again: Valery Majorov is back in the United States, last sighting yesterday, in New York."

"I'll mention that, if I have the opportunity."

"I'm sure you can find him."

"He didn't leave a forwarding address."

Lance hung up.

Stone checked his phone directory for the day before yesterday. Jack's calling numbers were blocked.

Joan knocked at Stone's door. "Got a minute?"

"Sure. Take a pew."

"Does that mean I'm going to get a sermon?"

"Merely a figure of speech, but you might."

"I'm going to sell my house." Joan had inherited major money and real estate from an aunt.

"Is twenty-two rooms not enough?"

"It's way too much. I bounce around like a pea in a rattle. I was happier next door."

Stone had bought the house next door some time ago, to house his staff. "I'm glad you still think fondly of us."

"How much should I ask?"

"Ask Margot Goodale." She was a Realtor Stone recommended.

"Who would want to buy the place?"

"Somebody with too much money and no impulse control."

"What, maybe fifteen, twenty mil?"

"Somewhere in there, would be my guess. It's like every other house. Somebody will like it and want it. It's Margot's job to see that he can afford it before he sees it."

"I guess."

"Have you thought of carving out a floor for yourself?"

"Even then, it's too much."

"Then God bless you and good luck."

"I'll call Margot." She went back to her office.

26

THE FOLLOWING MORNING, Joan buzzed him. "Ed Rawls, on one."

"Hey, Ed. How's the weather up there?"

"So-so, off and on."

"Is that the best weather report you can give me?"

"It's the best weather we got. It rained this morning, does that help?"

"It helps the roses, Ed."

"Makes me wish I had some roses. Whaddaya want?"

"That ear you keep to the ground—has it picked up anything lately?"

"From time to time, it picks up a vibe."

"What lately?"

"Russian lately."

"How solid a vibe is that?"

"Faint and indistinct."

"Still, it must be worth mentioning, since you're mentioning it."

"They may be hanging around. That's just a rumor, and not even a solid one. A whisper of a rumor."

"What are they up to?"

"It appears they're hunting."

"Not on Islesboro."

"Hereabouts."

"What's the prey?"

"You remember that dead guy they found on the ferry?"

"Yeah."

"He may not be as dead as we thought."

"He spent a night on my garage floor, packed in ice, and he never complained."

"That might have been some other guy."

"Why do the Russians mind about that?"

"Apparently, they prefer their dead people actually dead. You think that's unreasonable?"

"I guess not. Well, there is something to the rumor."

"Which one?"

"The not-quite-dead rumor."

"Where'd you get that?"

"From the horse's mouth."

"You sure it wasn't from the horse's ass?"

"It had teeth, a tongue, and could speak."

"How solid was the horse?"

"Pretty solid. I had dinner with him the night before last."

"And why do I need to know this?"

"He'll be landing there in an hour or two, in a V-tailed Bonanza."

"I hope he makes it through the gusts."

"It's okay. It's had the mod."

"Is he going to bother me?"

"He might, but he'll call first."

"He'd better, if he don't like holes in his head. Why's he coming?"

"He needs a rest, and he wants to get away from the Russians."

Rawls laughed aloud.

"And he heard that my house repels small-arms fire."

"That's the rumor."

"Lance says he heard a rumor that Valery Majorov is back in New York."

"He's a nasty piece of work."

"They all are."

"What does he want from this guy Collins?"

"His balls, apparently."

"Does anybody know why?"

"At least two people: Collins and Majorov."

"And what am I supposed to do about it?"

"You need some target practice?"

"Every day."

"It might be nice if Majorov got in your way."

"And then he takes a dip in Penobscot Bay?"

"Whatever works for you."

"There might be some pleasure in that for you."

"There might be."

"Are you coming up?"

"I'm planning to be somewhere else."

"Where?"

"Anywhere but there."

"That's antisocial of you."

"Maybe after the investigation is closed."

"Whose?"

"Maine's or Lance's, either one."

"I'll see what I can do. What's your man's phone number?"

"I don't have it. He'll be in touch with you."

"Okay."

"Buy the guy a drink for me," Stone said, then hung up.

27

JACK COLLINS WAS approaching Islesboro, but in fog, even at three thousand feet. He started down, planning one thousand feet at five miles. At two thousand feet, he was still locked in a white world. At fifteen hundred, he caught a glimpse of trees, and like magic, at one thousand feet he popped into clear air, with the airfield in sight. He turned wide downwind to land to the north and drifted down to seven hundred feet. That would keep him above the treetops. He got the gear down and put in some flaps as he made his turn to final. He aimed to miss the treetops and set down just past the runway numbers.

He taxied to the end of the runway, then turned around and taxied to the other end, looking for parked cars or men on foot in the trees. He appeared to be alone.

He spun around at an existing set of tie-downs, and ran through his shutdown procedure. With the prop stopped, he opened his door wide and listened. Silence.

As he was unloading his two suitcases, a 1938 Ford woodie station wagon pulled up to the airplane. He hadn't seen it coming. He adjusted his fake beard and moustache and hopped down from the wing, his hand out to meet Seth Hotchkiss.

From the north he heard a rumble of distant thunder.

"Looks like you made it just in time, Mr. Collins," Seth said. "It'll be raining hard in ten minutes."

"Please, Seth, it's Jack."

"Jack it is," Seth replied, tucking his luggage into the trunk.

As Jack slid into the passenger seat, he heard the thunder again, less distant than before.

Seth got in. "Are you tied down to your satisfaction?"

"I am."

The car began to roll, and shortly they were at the house. Rain began to come down, and hard. Seth pulled into the garage. "That door to the house," he said, pointing. "I'll get the bags."

As Jack stepped into the foyer, a clap of thunder nearly deafened him and lightning flashed. The house lights went off.

"Give it a few seconds," Seth said, "and the generator will kick in." It kicked in, and the lights came on again.

"We've got a full tank of diesel," Seth said, "and it will last a couple of weeks. The truck will be back by then, so we'll never go dark."

Jack followed Seth upstairs and into a guest room.

"Would you like some lunch?" Seth asked. "There's lobster stew."

"Thanks," Jack replied. "I'll be right down." The wind was gusting twenty or so knots now.

Downstairs Jack took a seat by the fire, and Mary brought him a tray and set it in his lap. "Would you like a glass of wine?" she asked.

"Yes, please."

She left, then returned with a glass. "Holler, if you need anything," she said, and left him to eat.

Jack could see out the back windows now, but not much further, what with the rain.

Somewhere a phone rang, and Seth called, "Stone for you, Jack."

Jack picked up the phone beside his chair. "Hello?"

"Did you beat the weather in?"

"Just barely," Jack replied. "I had it on the radar and stormscope ahead of time."

"Is your airplane securely tied down?"

"It is, thanks."

"Do you want to give me a phone number?"

"Sure." He recited it. "It's a throwaway."

"That's good enough. You might give Ed Rawls a ring when the weather is better."

"I'll do that."

"See you." Stone hung up.

Jack accepted a little more stew from Seth. "Anyone asking for me?" he asked.

"Nope, and if you stay out of the village store, nobody will."

"Stone had mentioned it."

He finished the stew and his wine, then he reclined his chair a bit and dozed through the thunder and lightning.

When he woke up, the rain had stopped, at least temporarily, and there were a few rays of sunshine outside. The phone rang again, and this time Jack answered. "Yes?"

"It's Rawls. Come down here at six for a drink, and if you're decent company, you can stay for dinner, which will be beef."

"Thank you, yes."

Rawls gave him directions to his place and instructions for dealing with the front gate, which apparently was a big log.

"See you at six," Jack said.

Seth came back in and gave him the keys to the Ford. "Can you drive a stick shift?"

"Sure."

"Not everybody can these days."

Jack went upstairs and changed for dinner.

28

Jack stared at the huge log across Rawls's driveway, and he was amused. Then the log/gate opened, he drove the Ford wagon in, and the log closed behind him. He was impressed.

As he approached the house the figure of a man appeared on the porch, clutching an exotic-looking rifle with a large scope mounted. Rawls waved him in, then pointed to a spot where he should park. He got out and received a perfunctory handshake.

"I'm Ed Rawls. All the awful stuff you've heard about me is probably true." He opened a door and waved Jack into the house and to a chair, then Rawls closed, bolted, and double-locked the door behind them. "It's my experience that fewer unwanted visitors come in if I do this. Booze?"

"Scotch, rocks, please."

"Single malt? I've got Laphroaig."

"Sure."

Rawls handed him the drink, then fell into the identical chair before the fireplace. "Cute disguise," he said.

"Thanks. Recently I've taken care not to be remembered by the people I meet."

"I've had days like that, too," Rawls said. "I should have seen your makeup artist."

"I learned a bit of it at the Farm," Jack said.

"I must have been hungover that day," Rawls replied. "Why do you think you need it on an island populated by about sixty people after Labor Day?"

"I don't know who the sixty are, and I'd rather they didn't know me, even by sight. Especially by sight," he added.

"Fair enough. I take it you've been warned about the village store?"

"I have."

"Jimmy's a nice fella, but once he's seen you, you might as well be on CNN. In fact, Jimmy is who CNN calls if they hear a rumor of news from up here."

"I'll miss my ice cream," Jack said.

"They've got Ben & Jerry's in cartons. Seth will bring your flavor."

"Good to know."

"I read your file," Rawls said.

Jack blinked. "I didn't know that was possible," he said.

"It's not, but I know my way around the super-computer. So, you see, I know what you look like at every age, since you were twelve, and from every angle, and with every attempt at a beard."

"I'm glad you're not a Russian," Jack said.

"So am I," Rawls replied. "In fact, I can't think of anything I'd rather not be. Which one's after you?"

"Majorov."

"Which one?"

"Valery."

"Every time I hear that name I think of the phrase 'nasty piece of work.'"

"That's the best description of him I've heard."

"Where did you first encounter him?"

"London, quite a while back."

"When Dick Stone was station chief?"

"Right. I did a couple of years under him. I was hoping he'd end up as director."

"He should have, and he was in line for it, but that was not to be."

"Spare me the details," Jack said. "I've already heard them."

"I'm relieved not to have to spit them out. How do you like your beef?" Rawls held up a hand. "If you're a vegetarian, you'll go home hungry tonight."

"Medium raw, please."

"That, I've got. The grill should be hot by now. Excuse me." Rawls got up, left the room, and came back three minutes later, looking at his watch. "I've got us a porterhouse. Takes half an hour. Anything you want to impress me with while we wait?"

"I don't think anything about me would impress you for five minutes."

"You forget, I've read your file. It's impressive, here and there."

"The gaps are probably more interesting."

Rawls freshened their drinks. "There oughta be a few gaps in every interesting file. Shows initiative and a fine disregard for authority."

"I'll cop to that last one," Jack said.

"Lance always favors those who did well at the Farm, and you did just fine. I think your continued presence on the planet is testimony to that."

"Thanks, I think."

"I hear you've got a nice wife."

"She was divorcing me until she heard I was dead, then she stopped."

"A lot of women would have kept right on going. You should have brought her up here. It's the only way you would get laid in these parts, at this time of year."

"I don't know. I hear you're keeping your hand in, so to speak."

"Oh, you can do all right, if your tastes run to sixty-year-old widows."

"I'll bet."

"They're not accustomed to a lot of attention."

"I'll keep that in mind."

"Of course, the only place you could meet them is in the village store, this time of year, the yacht club being closed."

"Maybe if I continue to wear my disguise," Jack said.

THEY HAD DINNER, and Jack enjoyed himself. It was nearly the only conversation he'd had since he was dead.

29

STONE WAS DOING the **Times** crossword the following morning when the phone rang.

"Yes?"

"It's Rawls. This late enough for you?"

"Eight o'clock," Stone said. "That's better than six."

"I had your boy over to dinner last night."

"And what did you think of him?"

"A bright young fellow, though not all that young. Everybody looks like a young fellow, when you're my age."

"Did you interrogate him?"

"I prefer to give a man some whiskey, then let him debrief himself. They don't feel cornered that way."

"What did you learn that I don't know?"

"Almost everything," Rawls said. "Looks like Lance Cabot sent him up here to deal with Valery Majorov, and somehow things went belly-up."

"How'd that happen?"

"Majorov was laying for him, but he picked the wrong victim."

"Who was the victim that got the two in the head?"

"Your boy's partner, so to speak. They had met only once, at the Farm, and Lance teamed them up."

"So Lance knows everything about everything?"

"He didn't at first. He thought Jack had taken the bullets."

"Who did Lance want to take the bullets?"

"Lance wanted a clean hit on Majorov, but he didn't get what he wanted. Instead, Jack's backup man, a guy named Jeff Burns, took the lead."

"And got himself cremated and scattered as a result?"

"Yeah, but Lance, apparently, didn't know that until after the remains had been dealt with."

"And when, in this scenario, did Jack emerge as the survivor?"

"Not until he was outta here, and back in New York."

"So Lance was twice surprised?"

"He was. He'd already written a letter of consolation to Jack's mother, but she turned out to be deceased. The letter was returned to Lance as undeliverable, and now it has to be forwarded to Burns's mother."

"So who's the bad guy in all this, if not Lance?"

"Valery Majorov, that's who."

"And he thinks he killed Jack?"

"As best as Jack can determine. I mean, two in the head is dead to a guy like Majorov. He's got somebody bleeding at his feet, that's where he expected Jack to be."

"Okay, I buy all that. But why did Majorov want Jack to be the dead guy?"

"Because in London a few years back, when Jack was working for your cousin Dick, he embarrassed Majorov in a major way—I'm not sure how—and Valery has a real good memory, never forgets anything, like an elephant."

"If his memory is so good, wouldn't he want confirmation that he offed the right guy?"

"I think we have to assume, for the moment, that Majorov thinks he killed Jack. Nobody has tipped him off, yet, about the identity confusion. This is why Jack is sporting a disguise."

"Why don't we assume—just for the hell of it—that Majorov has somehow figured it out. Does he still want to kill Jack?"

"He does." Rawls took a breath. "And you."

"Me? What do I have to do with all of this?"

"Apparently, Majorov just automatically assumes that anything bad that happens to him within, say, a thousand miles of your current location, is your fault."

"He holds a grudge, does he?"

"With a death grip. And my memory is that you have fouled up Majorov's existence half a dozen times. Or so."

"So I've been watching the wrong guy's ass all this time?"

"It would seem that the ass to worry about is the one you can hold on to with both hands."

"Any advice?"

"I think Jack came up here to find Majorov and kill him. Why don't you just give him time to do his work? And maybe get out of town while he's at it. And not here in Maine."

"That sounds like sane advice," Stone said.

"Sanity is my hallmark," Ed said. "Though there's them that think otherwise."

"England is nice this time of year," Stone suggested.

"Yeah, but not London. Majorov knows too many people there who know you. Same for Paris."

"You have a point."

"I usually do, and England seems like a good choice, as long as you stay out of the city and stay indoors. But then, you've always been a great indoorsman, Stone."

"Will you excuse me, Ed? I have some packing to do." Stone hung up.

30

STONE DIDN'T HAVE to pack much. After all, having a wardrobe at each of his houses was sort of the point, wasn't it? What needed to accompany him was a suitable person of the female persuasion. His first choice would have been Holly, but she traveled with one hell of an entourage. The only other choice was Vanessa, but she was loose-lipped, so he wouldn't be able to tell her anything. He called her.

"This is Vanessa."

"It's Stone. How would you like to get away for a week or two?"

"To where?"

"A pleasant place, the name of which you may not know, until we arrive, and maybe not even then."

"I like mysterious. How did you know that?"

"I guessed."

"And when do we depart?"

"My car will be at your door in sixty minutes."

"Holy shit! You expect a grown-up girl to be able to pack for an unknown destination and get down to the sidewalk in an hour?"

"Those are the arrangements."

"What clothes will I need?"

"Country, outdoorsy, along with a couple of nice dresses, in case somebody asks us to dinner—or we ask them."

"I think I can do it. I'll need to call the office."

"Call them from the car. Oh, and bring a passport, in case anybody gets curious about your nationality."

"I have to hang up now and start throwing things at suitcases. Any weight limitation?"

"Three large cases and a hanging bag and a cosmetics case."

"I'm wasting time talking to you."

"One hour."

"I know!" She slammed down the phone.

Stone had been prepared to give her an extra half hour, but, in the circumstances, her panic was his friend. He buzzed Joan.

"Yes, sir?"

"Tell Fred we're leaving for Teterboro in fifty-five minutes."

"So we're going somewhere?"

"Not we, me."

"Of course. I had forgotten that it is a condition of my employment that I never get to go anywhere."

"I need whatever pounds sterling are in the safe, and some real dollars, too."

"Sandwiches for travel?"

"Not necessary. Oh, call the Strategic Services hangar and tell them we need the airplane out of the hangar, wheels up in an hour. Oh, and you'd better let Faith know, too, since she's the pilot and needs to round up a copilot. I can fly right seat, if necessary."

"Destination?"

"Windward Hall, but don't tell a soul, except Faith, friendly or unfriendly. Tell Faith to expect to be gone for two weeks. Gotta run." He hung up. He ran for a shower and his clothes.

To HIS MILD astonishment, Vanessa was standing on the sidewalk with a pile of luggage when they pulled up. Fred made the bags go away, and she got in. "Whew!"

"I am impressed," Stone said, "to learn that I know a woman who can leave on time."

"May I know where we're going, please?"

"You may not, until we arrive."

"I hate not knowing," she said plaintively.

"I know you do, but it's absolute necessary for reasons of security."

"Whose security? Yours or mine?"

"Ours. You will appreciate it later."

Fred drove into the Strategic Services hangar at Teterboro and pulled up to the airstairs door of the Gulfstream 500. Faith and another woman in uniform were doing a thorough preflight inspection, and linemen were waiting to load luggage.

"Oh, it's bigger than I thought," Vanessa said.

"You'll be comfortable, I promise," Stone said, escorting her aboard and to a comfortable seat. A stewardess took their breakfast order and brought them mimosas and the **New York Times.**

Faith and her copilot boarded and entered the cockpit. Then the airplane began to be towed to the flight line. Outside, the tug disengaged, and the engines whined softly to life. Shortly, they were rolling again, taxiing to runway one. Without slowing, the Gulfstream turned onto the runway and full power was applied to the engines. Soon, the aircraft lifted off the runway and the landing gear were retracted with a soft thump.

"We are en route," Stone said.

"To what airport?"

"To no known airport," Stone replied, as breakfast arrived.

Vanessa looked out the window. "Is that Long Island out there?"

"Probably."

"So we're headed east?"

"Don't count on it," Stone replied.

31

B Y THE TIME they passed Montauk Point, Vanessa was asleep under a cashmere blanket, and Stone was halfway through the **Times** crossword.

Vanessa stirred. "All right," she muttered, "where are we going? Is it going to be a dirt track in the middle of nowhere? Somewhere on the frozen tundra of Iceland?"

"None of the above. The runway was built and operated in secret during World War II, to dispatch commando troops and spies. It has since fallen into my hands."

"Condition, please?"

"Seven thousand feet of well-maintained concrete."

"Not cement?"

"Cement comes in bags. It is mixed with gravel and water to make concrete, which is poured and smoothed."

"Is it in the middle of nowhere?"

"Au contraire. It is in the middle of a green and pleasant place."

"Ah, Ireland!"

"Close, but no Upmann. And that is all you may know until we land."

They had lunch and watched a movie, then the aircraft began its descent.

"We're coming down," she said, "but I still don't see any land."

"There is plenty of that where we are going. If you look to your left, you will see some."

"That looks very like England," she said.

"It is very like that," Stone replied.

As the sun set lower in the sky, trees and houses were visible, and they made a left turn.

"I caught a glimpse of a big house," Vanessa said.

"It is called Windward Hall," Stone replied. "It is where I repose when evil lurks elsewhere, like New York."

"Ah, that's right! You have a house in England!"

"You'll get a better view shortly."

The aircraft touched down softly, brakes were applied and engines reversed, then it made a 180-degree turn, stopped, and the engines wound down. A Range Rover pulled up to the bottom of the airstairs door, and as they descended, their luggage was loaded onto another vehicle, and Stone introduced Vanessa to Major Bugg. "The major is the estate manager, and nothing escapes his eye," Stone said, "so watch yourself."

"How do you do, Major?" Vanessa said, and shook his hand. Two officials from Customs and Immigration glanced at their passports and stamped them.

THEY WERE DELIVERED to the front door of the house and entered. "This is Windward Hall," Stone said. "We should go upstairs, unpack, and dress casually for dinner." He took her up a floor and showed her the master suite and her very own bath and dressing room. Then Stone sat her on the bed. "Now, listen," he said. "We are here because someone is trying to kill Jack, and failing that, we'll do nicely. Do you understand?"

"This isn't a trick, just to get me out of the country for immoral purposes?"

"Well, there is that, but the threat is real. Now, when you report to whomever you report to back home, like your mother, you must make no mention of this country, this house, or my name. If someone is inquisitive, tell them that we are at a remote location in the American West, sleeping by a campfire and riding horses. Nothing else."

"I understand," she said, "and I understand that you are serious and why."

"That is all I ask," Stone replied. "Well, I'll ask more later, when you've had time to digest that and are out of your clothes. Right now, it's you and me for dinner in the library. Freshen up."

HALF AN HOUR later they were having drinks on a Chesterfield sofa before a warming fire. The sound of rain could be heard pattering against the windows.

"It's raining," she said.

"It's England. It does that here."

"I recall that. When did you buy this house?"

"I bought it near the end of a two-year renovation, conducted by an interior designer, Susan Blackburn. The owner was ill and died soon after."

"I love England."

"You've been here before?"

"I have, and often, during my modeling days."

"We will not be reliving those, since our situation requires us to remain here, preferably indoors, unless we're riding. Do you ride?"

"I had my own pony when I was a little girl. I remember how."

Dinner was served: a tomato bisque, followed by a rack of lamb and fresh vegetables from the garden, followed by an apple tart with ice cream, all washed down with a bottle of Château Gloria, 1960.

"I'm going to fall asleep soon," she said, trying the dessert wine.

"Not before I have ravished you, I hope."

"I'll see what I can do."

As it turned out, she did just fine, before she lost consciousness in his arms.

32

THE FOLLOWING DAY it rained, off and on, and they contented themselves with a good lunch and reading from Stone's library. At mid-afternoon, Stone's cell phone rang.

"Yes?" he said cautiously, ready to hang up.

"It's Lance. That phone I gave you tells me where you are, but not with whom."

"I think it better not to mention it on the phone."

"I have a pretty good idea, anyway, and I approve."

"Thank you, Your Holiness," Stone replied.

"I'm glad that's how you think of me. Your sins, whatever they are, are forgiven."

"No Hail Marys?"

"About ten thousand, but we won't press the matter."

"Thank you again."

"The person you are hosting in a distant land has arrived, has parked his camels, and has been made comfortable by the reception committee."

"Oh, good."

"Our mutual acquaintance watches over him."

"Good luck to both of them, but I'm concerned only with my own ass and that of my companion. The others are on their own."

"I'll tell them you said so."

"Tell them whatever you like. I didn't get them into this mess."

"Sometimes a friend is a person who shares your enemies."

"I have no enemies, until they start shooting at me again."

"That event is not out of the question. I hope you realize that."

"Of course I realize it. Why do you think I'm here, instead of there?"

"You're a bit testy these days, aren't you?"

"You're lucky you're not here, where I could take a swing at you."

"Funny you should mention that: I'll be there for dinner tomorrow evening and a few days' stay. You might ask our mutual friend across the river to join us. Dinner is so much more fun when there are women about."

"Then I will supply them. I must return to my previous activity now."

"Of course, you must. Good day." Lance hung up.

Vanessa looked up from her book, something on décor, by Susan Blackburn. "Who was that? You didn't sound very happy to hear from him/her."

"That was Lance Cabot. He'll be here for dinner tomorrow night and for a few days' stay. I'll invite my neighbor to join us."

"Is he in the same business as Lance?"

"It's 'she,' and yes. Her name is Dame Felicity Devonshire, and she's the director of MI6, the British foreign intelligence service, which is analogous to the CIA."

"Oh, won't that be fun!"

"It may be. I think Felicity will find you attractive company."

Vanessa raised an eyebrow. "What are you suggesting?"

"Nothing, but Felicity might well suggest something. How do you feel about the attentions of other women?"

"That depends."

"I won't ask on what, but if you enjoy that sort of thing, the opportunity may present itself."

"Are you going to watch?"

"I would hope to do a great deal more than that, but I will follow your lead and Felicity's."

"Well, I'm glad you warned me. We'll see how it goes."

"Suffice it to say, I have no expectations, so I cannot be disappointed. And I've no objections to having you all to myself."

"As you have demonstrated so nicely, as recently as last night."

"And will continue to do so."

"Where does Lance come in, in all this?"

"He does not."

"What are his sexual preferences?"

"I don't know, and I don't think anyone else does, either, so you should not concern yourself. He can be good company at dinner, though, if he feels like it."

"I'm a good reader of people," Vanessa said. "By the end of dinner, maybe even after the soup, I will very probably be able to tell you what his preferences are."

"All this from across a dinner table?"

"Don't worry, I don't have to assault him to read him."

"Well," Stone said, "this could be fun." His cell phone buzzed, and he looked at it. "We may expect Dame Felicity at six-thirty tomorrow," he said.

"How am I dressing?"

"To kill. It will be black tie."

"Oh, good."

"I'm sorry you can't go shopping for a dress, but them's the rules."

"Fear not, I'm sufficiently stocked."

Stone's phone vibrated again, and he glanced at it and sent back a reply. "It seems the foreign minister, Sir John Parker, and his wife, Hillary, will be joining us for dinner. Felicity is putting them up at her house, so I should think that will put a damper on her intentions for after dinner. Sir John is, after all, her boss."

"Perhaps another time," Vanessa said.

"I believe that's what Felicity is thinking, too."

33

Stone came out of his dressing room and found Vanessa sitting on the edge of the bed, nude. He knelt and attended to things at the Delta of Venus.

Vanessa ran her fingers through his hair and sighed. "Who needs Dame Felicity?"

"We try to offer a complete service," Stone said, climbing atop of her. She lifted her knees to allow him full entry.

"And you do that so well," she breathed.

When they were both sated, they lay side by side. "Is anyone still trying to kill us?" she asked.

"Probably not," Stone replied, "but there's a loaded shotgun under my side of the bed, and a pistol in my bedside drawer."

"I know how to use both of those implements," she said, "in case I'm needed."

"Good to know. We might not have time for weapons instruction."

She fondled him. "I've already had weapons instruction," she said, "but I can always muster a second wind."

"I'm not sure I can," Stone said, "so let's save it for the morning."

They were both soon asleep.

THE FOLLOWING MORNING, Stone's eyes fluttered open, and he experienced a moment of disorientation, uncertain on what continent they were, but it was momentary. A birdsong outside snapped him into place; one didn't hear that often in New York.

"What kind of bird is that?" Vanessa asked.

"I've no idea," Stone replied. "My knowledge of ornithology extends only as far as robins and LBJs, as a friend of mine puts it."

"What's an LBJ?" she asked.

"A Little Brown Job," he replied.

She threw a leg over him. "I believe we have an appointment," she said.

Stone joined her. "I believe we do."

————

BREAKFAST WAS SENT up, and they had it in bed.

"You mentioned riding," Vanessa said. "Is that in the cards today?"

"If you will forgive me, I'd like us to stay indoors today, perhaps out of an overabundance of caution."

"I've no objection," Vanessa said. "Do we have to get out of bed?"

"Eventually, otherwise the staff will talk among themselves."

"Are they very talkative?"

"They are human, and thus talkative."

"And at what hour will our guests arrive?"

"Felicity at six-thirty, as will her guests, the Parkers. Lance is liable to turn up at any time, but I won't acknowledge his presence until the same time."

"Is Lance bringing someone?"

"Felicity will be his date, as it were. Have you ever met Lance?"

"A few times, with John."

"How did the two of you get along?"

"Well enough. Also, I may as well tell you, before Lance lets anything slip. I didn't actually meet John **after** his Farm days. We met there, where we were both in training."

"I don't know why I'm surprised," Stone said.

"I never fully joined the Agency. Wasn't for me, but it was good learning. I did become a model after, that wasn't a lie. Were you ever at the Farm?" she asked.

"Once, for two or three days. I'm still trying to forget the experience."

She laughed. "Oh, come on, it wasn't all that bad."

"The good days must have arrived after my departure. Once, however, I lost a bet and had to do the full course at the MI6 counterpart, in Scotland."

"How was that?"

"The weather was worse than at Camp Peary." She laughed.

"The weather is one of the few things you can count on, in Scotland."

"Did you learn anything?"

"Nothing that wouldn't have been covered at the Farm if I'd hung around long enough. The drill sergeants were equally odious."

"Sergeants are like that," she said. "I was there when Holly Barker did a guest lecture, you know."

"I did not know. How did she conduct herself?"

"Whip smart and a better shot than our shooting instructor."

"That sounds like her." He sought a change of subject. "How were you recruited?"

"Someone recommended me to Lance."

"Who?"

"Lance wouldn't tell me."

"You can ask him tonight," Stone said.

"I might just do that, if I can corner him for a minute."

"Cornering Lance is hard work," Stone said.

34

FELICITY AND HER guests arrived on time, being driven up from Stone's dock in a golf cart that was manned by a staffer.

Stone and Vanessa received them in the library and introductions were made.

Sir John Parker and his wife, Hillary, were a bit younger and more attractive than Stone had expected. He recalled that, not long before, Felicity had been in bad odor with the Conservative Party and thus with Sir John, but all seemed well now. And Felicity, apparently, more fragrant. Stone was not surprised that Felicity, who looked and was dressed gorgeously, had surreptitiously inspected Vanessa during the introductions and was impressed. Stone liked the idea of the two of them in bed with him.

Geoffrey, the butler, tended bar and filled orders, and finally, they were seated before the fireplace, with a cheery blaze going.

"Has the rain stopped?" Stone asked nobody in particular.

"It has," Sir John replied, "and according to the radar, for the evening."

"So you won't get wet either coming or going," Stone said. They continued in that vein until Lance Cabot joined them. He already knew everyone present.

"Ah, the widow Collins," he said to Vanessa.

"No, the divorcée Morgan," she replied. "I had begun the process before John was dead. We had nearly reached a property settlement, and so after he was resurrected, I allowed it to play out to the end."

"Clever girl," Lance said, careful to say it so that the others didn't hear. Stone read his lips.

"Good evening, Lance," Stone said.

"Ah, Stone! So good to find you hale and hearty. Any problems?"

"I thought you might know better than I."

"I noted that the front lights of the house were ablaze."

"They are on a timer and were ablaze the night before last, too, if anyone was interested."

"I parked my rental behind the house, so nothing will seem amiss to the casual observer."

"I'll avoid turning on the strobes and playing loud music," Stone said.

"Good idea."

"Stone," Sir John said, "the ministry is still buzzing with the tale of you driving Dame Felicity's brand-new Aston Martin into a river."

"I'm afraid that what you've heard is only the half of it."

"Details, please. I have much curiosity to satisfy back at Whitehall."

"Well, the ostensible reason for my being there was to drive the car back to Beaulieu for her, and someone there had suggested we do some timed driving around the place. I was doing quite well as I approached the river, when the car suddenly commanded itself to make a sharp turn to the right, driving us both off the bridge and into the river, finishing upside down, underwater."

"My goodness, what could have caused that?"

"A bullet from a Russian sniper into the right front tire did the job. I believe he was tracked down and dispatched a bit later. There will be more in your ministry's files than I know."

"And what became of the car?"

"I believe your ministry replaced it immediately."

"Well, that was before my time. I might not have been so generous."

"I'll keep that in mind whenever I drive one of Dame Felicity's cars."

Geoffrey called them to dinner at the other end of the room. Later, when they were done with cognac, Stone saw Felicity and the Parkers to their cart and joined Vanessa and Lance inside.

"Vanessa," Lance said, "could you excuse us for a moment, please? I'd like to speak to Stone about something."

"Of course," Vanessa replied. "I'm going to turn in."

When she had gone, Lance waited a moment, apparently to be sure that she was not listening at the door. "Stone," he said finally. "I want to bring you up to date on Jack Collins."

"Please do."

"Someone took a shot at him at the rear of your property, down by your dock."

"To any effect?" Stone asked.

"Well, yes. The shooter slipped up and made his presence known to Ed Rawls, who was on your boat, and Ed shot the man in the head, as is his wont."

"Any ID on the shooter?"

"No, before we could establish that, Ed had made the body disappear into Penobscot Bay. I would not have known about the incident had Jack not told me."

"So Jack is now on the alert?"

"Yes, but elsewhere. He took off in his Bonanza at dawn the next morning and flew God-knows-where."

"Well, at least he's safe, and Ed has another notch on his rifle stock."

"Yes, well, all's well that ends well, isn't it?"

"I expect that whoever sent the shooter may not think so. He might go on looking for Jack."

"Or you," Lance said.

"Why me?" Stone asked. "I was nowhere near there."

"But the shooter's employer doesn't know that. I expect he's curious to know."

"That's comforting," Stone said.

"I just want you to remain alert," Lance said, rising. "Now, if you'll excuse me, I'm off to bed."

Stone followed him as far as the top of the stairs, then let himself into the master suite. Inside, it was pitch dark.

Stone groped his way to his bedside lamp and switched it on, finding Vanessa and Felicity in flagrante delicto in his bed.

"I lost an earring and had to come back for it," Felicity said.

"Quite all right," Stone said, working on his buttons.

"Will you join us?" Vanessa asked.

"Continue as you were," Stone said, "while I shed some clothing." He left the lamp on, so he could find his way back.

35

STONE WOKE WITH sunlight streaming into the room and his bed empty of women. There were shower sounds from the guest bathroom.

Vanessa swept in, tying a dressing gown, with a towel around her hair. "You're awake!" she said, then sat on the edge of the bed. "Felicity crept out at dawn." She kissed him in a nice place. "Anything I can do for you?"

Stone stretched. "I believe everything that could be done for me has been done, twice."

"Lucky you."

"What does your day hold?"

"I believe you promised me a horse."

Stone checked the clock. "After breakfast," he

said. He called downstairs and ordered the food and the horses.

THEY GOT HOISTED into their saddles, she on the mare and he on the gelding. "After we start out, I want you to do something for me."

"There's more? And in the saddle?"

"Not that. You see the large manor house on our left."

"How could I miss it?"

"That is a country house hotel, belonging to our Arrington group of hotels. I want you to keep a close eye on it for people who make you feel suspicious or nervous, particularly for those bearing arms—rifles or shotguns. Alert me if you spot same. I'll take the right-hand side of our course, the wooded area. Be prepared to run your horse, but on no account dismount. We would be at a terrible disadvantage if we did."

"Got it. Did Lance say nothing to reassure you last night?"

"An attempt was made on Jack at my boat dock at the Maine house. As a result, he packed up and left. No one knows to where."

"I see."

They walked along, warming up their mounts. "Can you think of anyplace Jack might go, one with a runway? He's in his Bonanza."

"There's a hotel on a lake in the Adirondacks, one owned by the Rockefeller group. Called something like the Point. John is very fond of it and there's a convenient airport."

"Is it likely to be crowded this time of year?"

"Yes, with leafers, but he's unlikely to be seen by anyone who knows him."

"I'll pass that along, after Lance is out of bed."

"What time is it in New York?"

"Five hours behind. I'm tempted to roust him out of bed now. He's done that to me often enough."

"I had the strange feeling last night that Lance knew everything that was going on—about Felicity, I mean."

"I've found it best to assume that Lance knows everything about everybody and everything. You can't go wrong if you proceed on that basis."

"I'll keep that in mind. I was too far beneath him at the Farm to know such things."

They rode on down the fields toward the Solent. Stone pointed it out ahead. "That's the body of water that separates the Isle of Wight from the mainland," he explained.

"What's the Isle of Wight like?"

"Like a microcosm of England: fields and hills. I don't think we'll get over there this trip. The local yacht club, called the Royal Yacht Squadron, would be safe enough, but it sits on one side of the Parade, which is always filled with people, some of whom might have evil intentions."

"Another time, then."

"Right. It's very pleasant there. Did you see any suspicious characters on the ride down here?"

"Nary a one."

"Nor did I. Now let's see if we can get back to the stables without getting fired upon."

THEY RODE HOME at a gallop, right into the stable yard, where they gave the horses to the groom and went inside to the library for a drink.

"Something I forgot to show you," Stone said. He opened a panel next to the fireplace and showed her a pair of shotguns and a deer rifle. "Just in case," he said.

"Have you got something light in a handgun that I can carry?" she asked. "I'd like that better."

"Upstairs," he said. "I'll find you something when we go up to shower."

"I like this room so much," she said, curling up in a chair with her drink. "It's like something out of a Merchant Ivory film."

"Well put," Stone said, then dozed in his chair.

36

WHEN STONE AWOKE from his nap, Vanessa had been replaced by Lance, who now occupied a facing chair. He was doing the **Times** of London crossword, and quickly, which annoyed Stone, because he had never been able to get a single word on an English crossword.

"A good ride, I hope," Lance said, tossing the puzzle into the fireplace before Stone could rescue it for the answers.

"Yes, good. Things are so quiet here that I wonder if we haven't brought off this disappearance thing."

"Possibly, but in my experience, Russians are a patient lot. They're probably just sitting around, waiting for you to pop up, like one of those ducks at a carnival."

"Not a sitting one, I hope."

"Well, I had three guns, all sharpshooters, out there this morning, two in the forest and one in the Arrington, up high. They spotted nothing, somewhat to their disappointment. They had hoped for something to shoot at."

"Does that mean they believe that I'm not in England, or just here, in Hampshire? Can we safely pop up to London for a few days?"

"They may believe you're not here, but I wouldn't chance a trip to London just yet. Too many ways and places to get spotted."

Stone sighed. "Oh, well."

"Why can't you be satisfied with a little peace in this gorgeous place? Isn't that why you bought it?"

"Part of the 'why' is that it's close to London."

"Is this you or Vanessa talking?"

"It's all me. She hasn't said a word or dropped a hint. Do you think we'd be safe for a night in Cowes?"

"Probably, as long as you stick to the squadron. I'll come along and deal with your lines if you like."

"Good idea." Stone called Major Bugg and asked him to book marina space and rooms in the castle.

Vanessa came in, still in her riding clothes, but looking refreshed.

"Our fearless leader has approved an excursion

to Cowes," Stone said. "After lunch, pick out a dress."

"Oh, good," she said. "I was afraid you were getting bored."

"So was Lance."

AFTER LUNCH, EACH toting a bag, they set off in Stone's Hinckley 43 down the Beaulieu River. The weather was perfect, and the Solent was flat for the crossing. They pulled into the squadron's marina, and their lines were taken, then they walked the short distance to the castle. Inside, they were shown to their rooms, then went down to lunch in the ladies' dining room. A lot of boats on the Solent filled the view from their table, and they were nearly alone in the dining room.

Stone filled in Vanessa. "The Royal Yacht Squadron is the second-oldest yacht club in the world, having been formed in 1815. The oldest is the Royal Cork Yacht Club, in Ireland, formed in the eighteenth century, 1729, I believe. The castle was built by Henry the Eighth, to defend against the French, whom Henry distrusted, but it has never been fired on. The row of brass cannon out front are used for starting yacht races."

Lance's phone buzzed, and Stone shook his head. "Not in here."

"I'll just look at the text," Lance said, and

glanced at his phone. "You'll be glad to know that the coast is clear."

"Oh, good," Vanessa said.

"If we return to Windward Hall in one piece and without incident tomorrow, perhaps we'll hazard a jaunt to London," Lance said.

THEY DINED THAT evening in the members dining room, at a round table set for twelve, stared down on by fine portraits of past commodores, some of them kings. The décor was candlelight and old silver.

"What is the significance of the uniform all the men, except Lance, are wearing?" she surreptitiously asked Stone.

"It is the dress uniform, or mess kit, of the squadron, worn in the castle or on other formal occasions in a nautical setting."

AFTER THEY WERE done with the port and Stilton, they took their cognac on the front terrace, overlooking the starting cannon. No one shot at Stone.

37

THE FOLLOWING MORNING, Stone took Vanessa out onto the lawn, where they spread a blanket and watched the start of several yacht races, then they walked up to the pavilion for some lunch, where Lance joined them.

"I've made some calls," Lance said, "and I'm advised that Russians are thin on the ground in London, so if you want to go up for a couple of days, I think it will be all right."

Stone immediately phoned the Connaught and booked a suite. "Are you coming?" he asked Lance.

"All right."

Stone booked a room for him, too.

After lunch, they went for a drive around the island for a couple of hours, with one of Lance's cars staying a hundred feet behind them. They drove up to the Needles, the chalk rocks at the western end of the island, which had been worn down to lumps over the decades. Stone and Vanessa got out of the car and walked down to the big rocks and watched the waves break over them for a while. Then, as they turned to walk back to the car, Stone saw a man get out of Lance's pursuit car and dive to the ground, sighting his rifle.

Stone hurried Vanessa into the car, and they accelerated quickly. His cell phone rang, and he answered it.

"False alarm," Lance said coolly. "Some fellow with a shotgun out for rabbits."

"I'm glad your people are alert," Stone said, then hung up.

"Are we safe?" Vanessa asked.

"Yes, it was a false alarm; someone shooting rabbits."

"I'm glad we weren't the rabbits."

THEY DROVE UP to London the following day, uneventfully, with Lance riding shotgun and the pursuit car where it was supposed to be. They checked into the Connaught and ordered a room service lunch, then had a nap.

Later, Stone followed Vanessa up and down Bond Street where she deftly applied Stone's credit card to the stripping of half a dozen shops. They sent the boxes and bags back to the Connaught, where the concierge sent them up to their suite.

THAT EVENING, THEY had a drink in the hotel's American Bar, then strolled over to Harry's Bar, a restaurant a couple of blocks away, for dinner. They had Blinis, then ordered. Their first course had just been set before them when a man and a woman were seated at a table directly across the room from them. Stone thought the man looked familiar, but, he recalled, half the people in the world seemed to look familiar.

They were having their main course when the penny dropped in Stone's head.

"What's wrong?" Vanessa asked.

"Nothing," Stone said, reaching for his cell phone.

"Yes?" Lance said.

"It's Stone."

"And how is Harry's Bar?"

"As ever, except for one detail."

"What is that?"

"A man I believe to be Valery Majorov has been seated, along with a woman, at a table in front of us across the room."

"Are you certain?"

"No, since I've only seen the man once, a couple of years ago in Paris."

"Where are you in your dinner?"

"Our main course was just delivered."

"Finish it, sign your bill, then follow the head-waiter, who will take you to a rear door of the restaurant. You'll find yourselves in a garden."

"I know the place."

"Can you find your way back to the Connaught from there?"

"Yes."

"Keep it as casual as you can. Walk, don't run."

"Right." Stone hung up.

"Did you say that the man directly across from us is Valery Majorov?"

"Yes. Don't look at him. You'll turn to stone."

"I've already looked at him once, and I don't want a second glimpse."

"Then just look into my eyes," Stone said.

"Are you packing?"

"Yes," Stone replied.

"I'm so glad."

"Relax, Lance has given us exit instructions. Eat your dinner."

"I seem to have lost my appetite," she replied.

"Doesn't looking at me make you hungry?"

"Perhaps."

"We'll have dessert in our suite," he said, as the check was put before him. He added a big tip, signed for the bill, and rose. "Don't hurry," he said.

The waiter pulled out the table for them and

they followed the headwaiter to the garden door and stepped outside.

"How lovely," Vanessa said, looking around.

"Just follow the walk, and we'll take the first left."

She took Stone's arm and followed his instructions. Stone heard a door close behind them and held her back when she tried to hurry. They turned left and came out onto Mount Street and crossed it. The entrance to the Connaught was at hand, and they used it. A man followed them into the elevator, and Stone unbuttoned his jacket and felt for the butt of the pistol on his belt.

"Don't bother, old man," the man said. "I'm with Lance." The door opened, and in a moment, they were inside their suite. Lance awaited them before the fire, a cognac in his hand.

"Do sit down," he said.

They sat down, and Lance poured them a drink. "Was it Majorov?" Stone asked.

"I don't know. He was a passable double, though. You're not crazy, just a little paranoid." He took a sip of his brandy. "I think we'll go home tomorrow, though, just on the off chance."

38

THEY LEFT THE HOTEL EARLY, just after breakfast. Lance slid into the shotgun seat. "You're not paranoid," he said.

"What?"

"I talked with the headwaiter at Harry's Bar later. The man you saw was Valery Majorov."

"Oh, shit!"

"You made him correctly. The question is: Did he make you?"

"And what is your opinion on that?"

"He didn't look alarmed or make any phone calls," Lance said. "Still . . ."

"I don't know how good an actor I am," Stone said, "but I made a phone call—to you—and I may have looked alarmed."

"I thought you were pretty cool," Vanessa said

from the rear seat, which she shared with a lot of boxes and shopping bags.

"I guess we're about to find out," Stone said.

"Follow the white Mercedes estate wagon up ahead," Lance said. "There's another car behind us; they'll give notice of anything following us."

Stone put the Range Rover in gear and pulled onto Mount Street, following the white Mercedes some ways ahead. That car crossed South Audley Street, then turned onto Park Lane and went all the way around Hyde Park Corner twice, before peeling off and out onto Kensington Road.

"Go twice around the next roundabout, as well," Lance said.

Stone did so and left it pointing down the Southampton road. Fifteen minutes later they were on the motorway south. Lance's phone rang. "Yes?" He listened, then hung up. "There's a black BMW SUV behind our chase car that is of some concern. Proceed normally, and we'll see what happens. Leave the motorway at Southampton, instead of continuing on, and we'll try something else tricky." Lance made another call. "Follow the signs to the Isle of Wight ferry and don't stop, unless they make you. Drive aboard behind the Mercedes."

Five minutes later, they were aboard the car ferry, departing Southampton for Cowes. "Stay in the car," Lance commanded. "My people will have a look around."

Half an hour later, they were leaving the ferry and Cowes, and Lance directed Stone west, toward Yarmouth, while he made another call. Fifteen minutes later, they boarded another ferry at Yarmouth, then crossed the Solent to the mainland, then got off and made for Beaulieu. Lance was on the phone again.

Another quarter of an hour and they drove through the main gate at Windward Manor, then behind the house and into the large building that served as a garage.

"Inside through the kitchen door," Lance said, "while my people check out the grounds."

They were at lunch in the library when Lance got another call, listened, then hung up. "The black BMW followed us to the house, though they were too far back to see if we drove here. He went past the house to the end of the road, then made a U-turn and came back this way. By that time we were safely tucked away in the garage, then into the house."

"That was a circuitous routing," Stone said, "but clever."

"Thank you," Lance said. "Being evasive was always one of my better qualities. Now, can you order the airplane for takeoff at dawn tomorrow?"

"I can," Stone said, and called Faith. He hung up. "Wheels up at six o'clock," he said.

"We'll keep a close watch for bogies tonight," Lance said.

"Will you be flying with us?"

"I believe I will accept that invitation," Lance replied. "My boss likes it if I get a free ride now and then."

"Who's your boss?" Vanessa asked.

"I am," Lance replied.

39

THEY PACKED AT BEDTIME, Stone having little to pack. Someone came and got Vanessa's boxes and bags and put them on the cart for loading on the morrow.

"Well," Vanessa said, sliding into bed with Stone. "It was a brief visit, but an enjoyable one."

He turned to greet her. "And never more enjoyable than right here."

They enjoyed themselves again and fell asleep in each other's arms.

They were awakened for breakfast at five and boarded the airplane while the luggage was loaded aft. Lance sat up forward, so he could see the pilots.

Stone sat down beside him. "Do you fly, Lance?"

"Do you mean myself? With my hands on the controls?"

"Yes."

"No. I was trained for it but was too busy to keep up with the training schedule to stay current." Lance handed him a fresh copy of yesterday's **New York Times.** "The crossword is virginal," he said.

Stone joined Vanessa across the aisle and shared the paper with her.

"I see the **Times** has stopped printing John's death notice," she said.

"Lance probably checked the three-day option on the form, thinking that was enough to get the word into the air." He thought about that. "Still, there was the attempt on Jack at Islesboro, and that was after the notice ran."

"I wonder if they've found him yet," she said.

"Who, the Russians?"

"Da."

"I think Lance would have heard by now."

"You have a point," she said, filching the arts section, which contained the crossword, and burying her nose in a fashion piece.

They raced the sun across the Atlantic and called it a tie at Teterboro. The airplane was towed into the Strategic Services hangar, where they and their luggage deplaned. Lance had his own car waiting to take him to the heliport.

Back in the city, Fred dropped Vanessa and her goods at her building, where she gave Stone a grateful, luscious kiss, along with her thanks.

"Don't call until tomorrow," she said. "I'll be sleeping until then."

Fred drove to Turtle Bay and circled the block twice, before pulling into the garage and closing the door behind them. Stone's phone was buzzing as he sat down in his office.

"Dino for you on one," Joan said.

"Good afternoon," Stone said.

"You're back?"

"Only just at this moment."

"Dinner at P. J. Clarke's at seven?"

"Done."

They both hung up. Joan came into the office. "I hope it wasn't too much fun," she said.

"It was too brief to have been too much fun, but it was very pleasant."

"It's been quiet here. Various figures seemed to be casing the house the first couple of days. Then, I guess, they figured you had skipped town, so they vanished. Was there a reception committee on the other side of the pond?"

"An accidental one. We went out to dinner and the person we least wanted to see was sitting across the room. We don't know if he saw us, but we decamped this morning, just in case."

"I've had an offer on my house for twenty-two mil," she said.

"Tell Margot to throw a net over the bidder before he escapes."

"You mean I should accept the offer?"

"Immediately and with both hands."

"I'll instruct Margot." She went back to her desk.

Stone read his mail and returned his calls, then Joan came back. "Margot got him up to twenty-three point five mil, mostly furnished," she said. "And she's thrown a net over him. We close next week."

"I think you'd better put that check in the bank. Our safes here are full to overflowing with your cash."

"Oh, I've been slowly toting it to various banks. All that's left is your money."

He gave her back the sterling she had sent with him.

"Why, you hardly spent anything."

"Wait until you see the Amex bill," he said.

40

STONE GOT TO Clarke's a little early and found the bar less packed than usual. He took a seat, intending to save the next one for Dino, then he turned to the bartender, to receive his bourbon, which had already been poured. In that moment, the seat next to him was filled, and the occupant turned out to be more attractive than Dino.

She was, in fact, beautiful—a honey blonde with her hair around her shoulders, in a lovely dress that revealed cleavage, and there was much of it to reveal. "May I have a Macallan 18 on the rocks, please?" she said to the bartender, then turned to regard Stone.

"Put that on my bill," Stone said to the bartender.

She allowed herself a small smile. "You are very kind," she said, and there was a hint of an accent.

"I detect an accent," Stone said.

"You are very quick. I am Polish. Anna," she said, offering a hand.

Stone took it and found it strong and soft. "Stone," he replied.

"Like a rock?" she asked.

"Yes."

"You have a good hand," she said, squeezing.

"As do you," Stone said.

She gave him that little smile again, which caused a thrill to run down his leg. "I'm meeting a friend," he said. "Would you like to join us for dinner?"

"How kind you are. I'd love to."

"What brings you to New York?"

"Pleasure," she said, "along with a little business."

"What business are you in?"

"Vodka," she said. "My father makes Poland's finest. He sent me here to meet with someone who would like to be our North American distributor. I am to judge his worthiness and report back."

"How soon are you reporting back?"

"Not too soon. I still have pleasure to occupy me."

Dino had suddenly appeared and plugged into the conversation. Introductions were made. "That would explain why you are drinking Scotch, instead of vodka."

She made a face. "I drink vodka—Papa's vodka—all the time," she said. "Scotch is a nice change. Don't tell Papa."

"I won't tell Papa," Dino said.

"You can go home now, Dino," Stone said. "We won't be needing you anymore."

"Fat chance," Dino said.

"What does this mean?" Anna asked.

"No," Dino said. "I won't go home."

Anna gave him a big smile. "You are sweet, Dino."

They took possession of their table.

"What is good here?" Anna asked.

"Beef," Dino said.

They all ordered steaks, and Stone ordered an expensive cabernet, then they settled in.

"Have you met this distributor yet?" Stone asked.

"Yes, but he is old. At least forty."

Stone and Dino exchanged a glance. "Ripe," Dino said. "Like a good wine."

"If you say so," she said, trying hers. "Oh, I see what you mean."

Stone felt relieved.

She leaned over the table, exposing more cleavage. Stone and Dino were transfixed.

"What is Papa's vodka called?" Dino asked.

"Polska. They will not have it in this restaurant until I choose a distributor."

"We'll hold our breath," Dino said.

Their steaks came, and they ate—Anna, greedily, as if there were a shortage of beef in Poland. Stone ordered a second bottle of wine.

"If you will excuse me," Anna said, "I must visit what you call, I believe, 'the little girls' room.'"

Stone and Dino stood, so the table could be moved, then they both watched her walk away, an uplifting experience.

"I've got a big disappointment for you, pal," Dino said.

"What's that?"

"She's not Polish."

"And why do I care?"

"You should care that she's lying. She's Russian."

"So?"

"So what is the nationality of the people who are trying to kill you?"

Stone started to speak, and his jaw dropped.

"I'll say it for you," Dino said. "Russian."

"How can you tell?"

"Something about her tits."

"I heartily approve of those."

"Who could not, but it's her handbag that worries me."

"Dino, why would I give a shit about her handbag?"

"Because she's packing," Dino replied.

"Dino . . ."

"And she's going to come out of the 'little girls' room,' walk up to this table, shoot you in the head, and walk out."

"You're just trying to get her all to yourself. I'll tell Viv on you."

"Viv would have made her first—and would probably already have shot her. Why haven't you gotten out of here?"

"What about you?"

"I'll stay here and stall her for a minute, while you run like a deer."

"This is insane," Stone said.

"It worked, didn't it?" Dino looked up. "Uh-oh. Too late." He reached under the table for something.

Anna was striding out of the ladies' room and into the dining room. She sat down but did not put her handbag on the table.

"Listen for a moment, Anna," Dino said, "and tell me, what do you hear?" He cocked the snub-nosed .38 he used for a backup.

Anna's face froze.

"Place your handbag and both hands on the table," Dino said.

She thought about it for a millisecond, then complied.

Dino produced a pair of handcuffs. "Cuff her," he said to Stone.

"You're not kidding?" Stone said.

"I kid you not."

Stone reached over and cuffed her.

Dino opened her handbag and dumped its contents on the table. The contents included a Beretta .25 semiautomatic pistol and a spare magazine. There was a short silencer screwed into the pistol barrel.

"Anna," Dino said, "it is a felony to possess a handgun in this city without a carry license. It is punishable by a prison term and it is another felony to possess a silencer. You are under arrest." He showed her his badge, then handed his .38 to Stone, and took out his cell phone. "Shoot her if she moves, and she probably will."

Stone leveled the weapon at Anna. "Then I will certainly shoot her."

Dino pressed a button and spoke into the phone. "Come in here with a weapon drawn and ready to make an arrest," he said.

While they waited, Dino returned her belongings to her handbag, sans weaponry, and tucked it under her arm. "You can call the number they give you when you arrive at the precinct, and they'll send a lawyer, but you should expect to remain in jail until your trial, a few months, since you are a threat to the public safety and a flight risk."

Anna, who had not spoken since returning from the little girls' room, spoke. "I wish a lawyer," she said.

Dino's driver came in and took charge of the prisoner.

"We'll be along in a few minutes," Dino said to him. "Lock her down, but first, have a female detective conduct a full cavity search, and check her hair for a hatpin. Let everybody know that she is very dangerous."

Stone spoke up. "Can I have thirty minutes alone in a cell with her, cameras off?"

"If you do that," Dino replied, "she'll try to kill you, and she knows how." He shoved the check across the table. "Dinner is on you," he said.

41

Dino and Stone got into the rear seat of Dino's armored GMC. "Let's drift up to the 19th Precinct and see how our guest is doing," he said to his driver.

"No problems getting her there," the driver replied. He drove uptown for the few blocks. As they approached the precinct, they saw an ambulance parked out front, its blue light spinning. Two men and a woman came down the front steps with a gurney. The woman was holding an IV bag above the patient, who appeared to be another woman. They got her into the ambulance, and it drove away.

Dino hit the sidewalk running and went upstairs into the precinct, with Stone hot on his heels.

"Commissioner," the desk sergeant said, "one flight up."

They were met by a man in a suit and tie, minus the jacket, holding both hands up. "Commish, it's all under control."

"**What** is under control?" Dino shouted at the man.

"The perp had a handcuff key on her somewhere. Detective Rosie Mack took her into a holding cell for the body and cavity search, there was some noise, and the perp came out of there with her hands free and Rosie's piece in one of them. She grabbed her handbag from my desk and made it down the stairs without shooting anybody, took an unmarked cruiser, and drove it away. I've issued an APB."

"What is the extent of Rosie's injuries?"

"She was stuck in the chest with something smaller than a knife and hit on the back of the neck. She was unconscious, and there was some blood."

"Where's she headed?"

"Lenox Hill ER."

"Has anybody reported the cruiser?"

"No, sir. It's a Toyota four-door, gray."

"Let's go," Dino said to Stone and ran down the stairs. "Lenox Hill ER," he said to his driver.

"What about the cruiser?" Stone asked.

"With a one-car search party, we're not going to find it. Leave it to the net; I want to see Rosie."

They got out of the car at the ER entrance and ran inside. Dino brushed a nurse out of the way and started looking in examining rooms.

Another nurse stopped him. "She's on her way to the OR with a small puncture wound to the heart and a concussion."

"Was she conscious at all?"

"Briefly. She said something about a hatpin and a headache, then she passed out."

"What are her chances?"

"Good, but they've got to crack her chest, so she'll be down for some time."

"No point waiting," Dino said. "Tell her I was here, and when she shows signs of waking up, call me immediately." He handed the nurse a card. "No matter what time it is." He stalked out of the ER with Stone on his heels.

"As I recall," Stone said, "you and Rosie were sort of an item a while back."

"A long while back," Dino said. "But she's a great person, and I love her as much as I love anybody but Viv. She didn't deserve this, and I'm going to find out why my instructions weren't followed to the letter."

They arrived at Stone's house and the driver pulled into the garage, per Stone's instructions.

"Do I have to tell you to watch your ass?" Dino said. "I mean, she came for you."

"No, you don't have to tell me."

"I'm going to put a uniform on your front and

rear doors, until you can get Mike Freeman at Strategic Services to get some people over here. I hope I don't have to tell you that she walked into a crowded bar, suckered us both, and damn near committed two murders."

"Why would she go after you?" Stone asked.

"Because I was there, and I made her. She wouldn't have hesitated. This is who you're dealing with."

"I understand, believe me. You want to wait here for the call?"

"I may as well. Viv is in the Far East somewhere for another couple of days, and I'm glad she is."

"Coffee?" Stone asked.

"Nah, I'll catch forty winks on your office sofa. You go to bed. I don't want you cluttering up the ER when Rosie comes out of it."

"All right. Call me after you've seen her, and give her my best."

"Yeah, sure. She'll like that." Dino headed for Stone's office and slammed the door behind him.

Stone went upstairs, stripped, and fell into bed.

42

STONE CAME DOWNSTAIRS the following morning and was surprised to find Dino still in his office. "Have you seen Rosie?"

"She's awake, but they won't let me see her until the surgeon has conducted his post-op examination. They told me to come at ten o'clock."

"Have you dismissed your driver?"

"Yes, I sent him home for some sleep."

"Then we'll take my car." Stone picked up the phone and asked Fred to get it ready to leave the garage. At 9:30 they got into the Bentley, and Fred opened the garage door and drove out. The traffic was heavy, and it was ten o'clock before they got out of the car at Lenox Hill. A nurse took them upstairs, and the surgeon was leaving

Rosie's room as they arrived. Dino introduced himself. "How is she?"

"She's had a rough night. Although we made the repair without difficulty, she's picked up an infection, and we're treating her with intravenous antibiotics."

"But she's going to make it, isn't she?"

The surgeon's brow wrinkled. "I suspect that the needle she was stabbed with was infected with something."

"Deliberately?"

"Most likely. We're waiting for the antibiotics to kick in now."

"May we see her?"

"For just a moment, if she's awake." The surgeon nodded to a nurse, who led them into the room and to Rosie's bedside.

Rosie's eyes were closed, but they fluttered as Dino spoke her name.

"Dino?"

"I'm right here, baby; Stone is here, too."

Rosie spoke with some difficulty. "It was the wig," she said.

"Her hair was a wig?"

Rosie nodded. "I think . . . I think the key and the needle were hidden under the wig." Then she closed her eyes and seemed to sleep again.

The nurse took Dino by the wrist and elbow and forcibly escorted him from the room. He and Stone sat down on a bench.

"Did you make her hair as a wig?" Dino asked.

"It never crossed my mind," Stone replied. "Good place to hide something small like a handcuff key and a hatpin, though."

"It also means that we're not going to find her anytime soon. Her appearance will be too different. And if she or whoever's running her is that smart, it means she was in a safe house very soon after she left the station. I forgot to tell you. They found the cruiser she stole parked next to the Lexington Avenue subway stop at Sixty-Third Street. She could have taken the train uptown or downtown."

"Or she could have left the car there, got rid of the wig, and hoofed it to the safe house. Let's go back to my place and have some breakfast. They'll call you when she wakes up again."

"Okay, I don't know how much more Rosie could tell us, anyway."

THEY HAD A good breakfast and were on coffee when Stone's cell phone rang.

"Hello?"

"It's Lance. How's the detective doing?"

Stone told him everything he knew.

"That's all very clever, isn't it?" Lance asked.

"Too clever for a Russian crime boss?"

"It smells more like an intelligence service."

"If you say so."

"Except what motive would an intelligence service have for wanting you and, possibly, Dino dead?"

"And what crime boss would try it at P. J. Clarke's, at dinnertime?"

"I'm going to have to take a deeper interest in this," Lance said.

"Welcome aboard," Stone replied. "We're certainly not getting anywhere."

"Now the attempted murder of Jack Collins looks more like something planned by an intelligence service, too. I mean, all three of the potential victims are associated with us."

"Any suggestions?"

"Yes, I'd like for you and Dino, if you can persuade him, to move into rooms at our New York station, where we can seal you off from anything that might be out there."

"No, thanks. I'm not moving into some federal motel for the duration. You can seal me off at home—if you think you can do it."

"Have you talked to Mike Freeman at Strategic Services yet?"

"Only in passing."

"I'll call him and work out a plan. In the meantime, don't answer your door for anybody, male or female. And tell Joan to tell anybody who calls that you've gone up to Maine for a few days."

"All right."

"Talk to you later."

Stone hung up and buzzed Joan to come into his office. "We're under siege here, sort of," he told her. "Nobody gets into the house until after the Strategic Services people get here to screen them. And all callers are to be told that I've gone to the Maine house for a week or so."

"Right, boss," Joan said.

"And I don't want you leaving the two houses at all for a while. Fred can deal with groceries."

"Oh, good, I can sleep all the time, or watch old movies on TV."

"Nope. You still have to work. You just have to do it indoors and on the phone."

"Oh, all right. Have you told Lance about this?"

"Yes, and he's the reason I'm taking all this so seriously."

"Then I guess I'd better, too." She went back to her office.

43

THE STRATEGIC SERVICES TEAM, led by their boss, Mike Freeman, arrived and went carefully through the house, checking the electrical, phone, and security systems for anomalies or intrusions. Then they assigned people to posts around the house. When they were done, Stone and Dino sat down in front of the fire in the study and had a drink.

"You want to get out of town?" Stone asked.

"What did you have in mind?"

"Well, in this country we have Los Angeles and Key West available. I think we've blown England for a while, and Lance says there are too many Russians in Paris for us to feel safe there."

"Can we wait until Viv gets back tonight and

check with her? She should be at home and in bed by around ten this evening."

"Sure. Tell her she gets to choose."

Stone called Vanessa.

"Hey. How you doing?"

"Not so good," Stone said. "A woman tried to kill Dino and me at Clarke's last night, and she seriously injured a detective after Dino had her arrested."

"Good God! You'd better stay away from women."

"That's too difficult a cure," Stone said. "Dino and I were just talking about abandoning New York for a bit. He wants to talk to Viv about it when she gets home tonight. Are you up for more travel?"

"Where did you have in mind?"

"At the moment, the choices are L.A. or Key West."

"I've never been to Key West."

"Have you been talking to your ex-husband?"

"Nope. Haven't heard a word."

"Try and keep it that way, until we figure this out."

"Okay."

"Not a word to anybody."

"I swear."

"I'll call you when Dino has talked to Viv."

"I'll stay by the phone." The both hung up.

"Vanessa is good to go—just about anywhere, I think."

They were nearly ready for dinner when Viv called Dino, and they chatted for a while. Dino hung up. "Viv is good for Key West, but she'd like to wait until the day after tomorrow, so she can clear her head of the jet lag."

"Okay, wheels up at ten AM the day after tomorrow."

"You're on," Dino said.

Stone called Vanessa and gave her the news, and she was on board for the trip.

"We'll snatch you off the curb at nine AM sharp, day after tomorrow," he said.

"I'll be there."

Stone called Joan and asked her to alert Faith and her crew, then Dino turned their attention to dinner, which Fred was serving.

STONE PACKED LIGHTLY, then got into the car to pick up the Bacchettis and Vanessa, who lived in the same building. When he arrived, Vanessa's luggage was sitting under the building's awning, and he asked her doorman to load it into the Bentley. Viv and Dino appeared and loaded up.

Stone went to see the doorman at the desk. "Heard from Ms. Morgan?" he asked the man.

"No, sir. I brought her bags down, but that was fifteen minutes ago."

"Call her, please."

The doorman rang her apartment, waited, then hung up. "No reply, Mr. Barrington."

Stone went and got Dino. "Get the doorman to give you a key to Vanessa's apartment." Dino did so, and they took the elevator to her floor. They stepped into the vestibule outside her door.

"Are you packing?" Dino asked.

"Yes."

"Then get it out. I don't like this."

Stone took out his .380, pumped a round into the chamber, and set the safety.

Dino put the key into the lock and turned it slowly, then nodded to Stone. He pushed open the door, and Stone went in first, with Dino right behind. They cleared the kitchen and the living room, and Dino went toward the bedroom. "In here!" he shouted, and Stone joined him.

Stone found Dino in the bathroom, kneeling over Vanessa. There was blood on the floor.

"She's done," Dino said. "This probably happened while we were loading the luggage."

Dino picked up the house phone.

"Yes, sir?"

"There may be a man or woman coming down the service stairs. Don't interfere with them, but watch to see where they go and get a license plate, if you can. The police will be here momentarily."

Stone called 911 and made a standard report, then they went and sat in the living room to wait for the detectives to arrive.

"This is bad," Dino said. "We're consistently underestimating these people."

44

STONE REMAINED IN the living room to talk to a detective, while Dino went back to the crime scene to talk to the detective's senior partner.

"Who went through the door first?" the detective asked.

"I did."

"By how much?"

"By seconds. The commissioner was right on my heels. It was he who found the body, in the bathroom, while I was clearing this room."

"Were you armed?"

"We both were."

"Let me see your license."

Stone gave it to him, along with his detective

first class retirement badge. He cleared his pistol and handed it to the detective.

"You didn't fire it?" the man asked, sniffing at the barrel.

"No, there was nothing to fire at. The perp must have been headed downstairs."

"Is there a back elevator?"

"Yes," Stone said, pointing. "And back stairs, too. Dino called the doorman immediately and asked him to look for anyone departing the building."

"Does the doorman carry, as a matter of routine?"

"I don't know. You'll have to ask him. Or Dino. He might know. He lives in the building."

"Where's the commissioner's wife?"

"She was waiting downstairs in my car. She may have come upstairs."

"Well, Mr. Barrington, you look clean for this one."

Stone glared at him. "I'm always clean. I'm not a criminal, and I won't be treated as one."

"That's right," Dino said from the doorway behind Stone. "By the way, I'm clean, too."

"Sorry, Commissioner." The doorbell rang, and he went to answer it. Dino was right behind him. He came back. "That was the medical examiner. He's on the job now."

The senior detective sat down next to Stone. "A few questions," he said.

"Of course."

"How would you describe your relationship to Ms. Morgan?"

"We've been seeing each other socially, and we have traveled together. We were on the way out of town with the Bacchettis when this happened."

"Where were you headed?"

"To Teterboro Airport."

"And from there?"

"I think Dino has probably told you: that's confidential."

"Yeah, he mentioned that. He didn't say why."

"You heard about Rosie, at the precinct."

"Yeah."

"That's why. The woman who hurt Rosie already made an attempt on my life and Dino's."

"The Polish woman?"

"More likely, the Russian woman."

"Any news on her?"

"No, and there's not likely to be. She's clearly a pro, and she's gone to ground."

"You think she did this?"

"I wouldn't be shocked to learn that she did. Still, she wouldn't be walking the streets. I don't think she would have been available for this. There's probably another pro in the picture."

Dino walked into the room in time to hear this exchange. "We can't rule her out," he said. "She has the qualifications, and she's loose."

"I can't deny that," Stone said.

The ME came in. "Time of death, half an hour ago. Cause of death, a thin needle to the heart, while being strangled."

"Then it was Anna," Stone said. "That was the name she gave us. She tried the same thing on Rosie, but failed to get it done."

"Description?" the detective asked.

"Great question," Dino said. "She was heavily made up and bewigged," he said. "I can't even tell you how tall she stood, but I'm guessing five-eight, on her feet. She was wearing heels at Clarke's. She wasn't skinny; she was very well equipped. God knows what she looks like now, or what she'll look like tomorrow."

Stone and Dino left the scene with Viv, who had joined them at the apartment while they were talking with the detectives. They took the elevator down.

"Are you going to order a search of the building?"

"No, she probably had the place cased. She'd have taken the elevator to the basement and walked out up the alley to the street and into a cab."

"Figures," Viv said. "I didn't see anybody leave the building when I was sitting in the car."

"Now what we have to do is decide where to go," Stone said.

Viv thought about it. "Do you have any reason to believe that Majorov's people know about your house in Key West?"

"No," Stone said.

"Then I think we should continue our trip, as if nothing had happened."

"I've got to deal with Vanessa's body."

"You can do that on the phone or let Lance deal with it. She's one of his, after all."

"Good point," Stone said.

45

Back in the car, Stone called Faith.

"Yes, sir?"

"Change of plan: move the airplane to Westchester County Airport and file for Palm Beach International. We'll change our destination en route."

"Got it."

Stone called Lance on his private encrypted line.

"Cabot," he said.

"It's Stone. What have you heard?"

"Nothing. What are you talking about?"

"Dino, Viv, Vanessa, and I were about to depart for points south. We stopped to pick up Vanessa. Dino and I went up to her place and found her on the bathroom floor, bleeding. The EMTs weren't able to bring her around. The ME says the technique was the same as used on Rosie."

"Well, shit," Lance said.

"Have you located Jack Collins?"

"Nearly, not precisely."

"Somebody needs to attend to Vanessa's body."

"Where is she?"

"City morgue, by now."

"I'll deal with it from this end. Are you headed where I think you're headed?"

"Yes."

"I think that's the safest place you can be right now."

"That's what we thought."

"I'll speak to you later, hopefully with news of Jack." Lance hung up.

"Lance is on it," Stone said, hanging up. "He thinks Key West is the right place to be."

"Where's your yacht?" Viv asked.

Stone grabbed his phone. "Why didn't I think of that?" He dialed another number.

"This is Captain Todd."

"Todd, it's Stone Barrington."

"How are you?"

"I'm okay, where are you?"

"At the old submarine base."

"We're on our way there now, ETA in about four to five hours. Can you take us aboard?"

"Certainly. How long a cruise?"

"Maybe a week."

"We'll be ready for you. Do you want to be met? We have the van."

"Sure, we'll be at our hangar. Meet us inside." He hung up.

"**Breeze** is at the sub base. The captain is picking us up in the van at my hangar."

Dino was asleep, so they didn't wake him with the news. Stone settled in with the **Times** crossword.

THE GULFSTREAM 500 was ready at Westchester County Airport in White Plains, New York. They boarded immediately while the ground crew dealt with the luggage. Fifteen minutes later, they were rolling down the runway.

"I feel better now," Viv said.

"So do I, except about Vanessa."

Stone drifted off and didn't wake up until he felt the airplane in a right turn. They would be direct to Key West. And if, by any chance, Majorov knew about the Key West house, he wouldn't know what was waiting at the old sub base. Because Stone had had, as guests, three presidents, the Navy had given him the use of a berth there. He fell asleep again, and didn't wake up until he felt the airplane's landing gear come down and lock into place, with the resultant reduction in airspeed. He picked up the phone and buzzed Faith.

"Yes, sir?"

"Head for our hangar. We'll deplane inside."

The airplane turned left off the runway and followed a golf cart with a sign on the rear that read FOLLOW ME.

Stone surveyed the airport from his window and didn't see a threat of any kind.

THE MERCEDES SPRINTER van dropped them at **Breeze**'s gangplank, and they went into the saloon immediately, while the crew dealt with the luggage. Stone ordered a round of vodka gimlets, his standard drink in tropical climates, and they sat down. "Vanessa," he said, raising his glass. Dino and Viv echoed his toast, and they took their first sip of Key West.

The skipper came into the saloon. "What's our plan?" he asked.

Stone looked up. "Can we make Fort Jefferson by dark?"

"No, but there's a nice anchorage on the way there that we can make by sunset."

"Let's go there," Stone said. "We're on the lam, and we don't want to be seen by anybody."

"Then you should stay indoors until we're well clear of the harbor," the skipper said. "Dinner at eight, okay?"

"Perfect," Stone said. "On deck, if it's not windy."

46

W HEN THE SUN was low in the sky, everyone went below to freshen up. Stone was getting into clean clothes when there was a rap on his door. "Come in."

Viv was at the door. "I just wanted to know if we're actually 'dressing,' i.e., black tie."

"No," he replied.

"What's that?" she asked, pointing. "It's not yours, is it?"

Stone followed her finger to a suitcase. "No, it's Vanessa's," he said. "They must have loaded it into the car when we stopped to pick her up."

"What's in it?" she asked.

"Her clothes, I guess."

"Do you mind if I have a look in it?"

"No, and I don't think Vanessa will mind, either."

Viv put the case on Stone's bed and tried to open it. "Locked," she said. "I'll be right back." She left Stone's cabin and returned with a small, zippered bag.

"What's that?" Stone asked.

"Oh, just a few burglar's tools. You'd be surprised how often they come in handy on the road." She tried a couple of tools, and the locks, one by one, snapped open.

Stone watched as Viv removed a pile of clothing with both hands, then stopped. "Well," she said, "this is interesting."

Stone walked over and looked into the bag. "What is it?"

"It's my guess that it's somewhere around a million dollars in cash," she said, holding up one of a number of bundles. She also grabbed a pistol. "We've also got a silenced 9mm pistol, along with three loaded magazines, and a very sharp field knife." She held up the weapons. "And," she said, picking up a gray box, "an apparent bomb made of about six ounces of military-grade plastic explosive and a cell phone. I'd better be sure it's not armed."

"Would you mind performing that task on deck?" Stone asked, getting into his deck shoes and grabbing a sweater. He followed her on deck.

She laid the box down on the coffee table and went to work on it with her tools. "Cell phone," she said, holding one up and unplugging it from the bomb. "There, it's inert now."

"Thank you, Viv," Stone said. "Oh. And thank you for all that money on my bed."

Dino had followed them up the companion-way and was inspecting the bomb. "Holy shit," he said.

"I've disarmed it," Viv said.

"And what's this about money on the bed?"

"Why don't you go down to my cabin and count it," Stone said.

Dino went below for about ten minutes, then returned with a zipped leather envelope. "I make it about a million two," he said, holding up the envelope. "Then there's this." He unzipped it and shook the contents out onto the coffee table. "Three passports," he said. "All with Vanessa's photograph. American, Canadian, and—wait for it—Russian."

"I would guess from the contents," Viv said, "that Vanessa hadn't planned to return from Key West with us."

Stone sat down on the afterdeck and collected himself. "I need a drink," he said.

Dino brought them all one and sat down. "I think you'd better call Lance," he said.

Stone tried and failed. "No service out here."

"Use the satphone."

"That's insecure. I'd better wait until we pick up a cell tower, maybe at Fort Jefferson."

"Good idea," Dino said, tossing the passports onto the dining table. He shook the envelope again and a small, black object fell out.

"What's that?" Stone asked.

"A tracker," Viv said. She took a small hammer from her tool kit, set the object on the deck, and hammered it until it was in pieces. Then she scooped them up, walked to the rail, and dropped them overboard. "Or it was," she said.

Suddenly, the unexpected: Stone's CIA encrypted phone rang. "Yes?"

"It's Lance."

"Reception is bad. We may lose you."

"Where are you?"

"Out of Key West, halfway to Fort Jefferson."

"Say again."

Stone repeated himself.

"Call me back when you have lots of bars," Lance said, then hung up.

"Signal failed," Stone said. "We'll try again tomorrow."

A crewwoman materialized. "Dinner's in half an hour," she said. "It's Boeuf Wellington, new potatoes, and haricots verts. Gazpacho to start."

"Fine," Stone said, and she left.

"You don't look so good, Stone," Viv said.

"That goes with how I feel," he replied. He excused himself, walked to the rail, and vomited overboard.

"There," he said, "that's better."

47

THEY FINISHED UP dinner with Key lime pie and coffee. They had not discussed the contents of Vanessa's bag or her intentions.

"Okay," Stone said. "What do you deduce from the evidence at hand, Viv?"

"You mean, Vanessa's Girl Scouts spy kit?"

"For want of a better term."

"I think it originated with one of three sources," she said. She held up a finger. "One: Valery Majorov. Two: Lance Cabot. Three: whatever they call the Russian spy agency these days."

"I like KGB," Stone said. "It has a nice ring to it, and I can't remember what part of the alphabet they're using to describe it these days."

"Your choice?" Viv asked. "Or something else entirely?"

"Come back to me," Stone said.

"Dino?"

"Valery Majorov."

"Me, too. Stone?"

"I think Vanessa put it together from whatever her ex-husband left behind in his safe."

"You think he had a million two in his safe?" Dino asked.

"I know he had more than that in an offshore account with a Cayman bank, and Vanessa had the necessary codes to draw on it."

"And the bomb?" Viv asked.

"You've got me there. Maybe Jack intended to blow up something or somebody."

"Any candidates for blowing up?" Dino asked.

"Just one: Valery Majorov."

"That seems a cumbersome way to off a Russian," Viv said. "I mean, there was a knife and a gun in the package, too. Either would have worked just as well and would have left a lot less debris and collateral damage to innocent passersby."

"Good point," Stone said.

"A good question to ask," Dino said, "is: Why would Vanessa bring a bomb with her to Stone's house in Key West?"

"Maybe it was the last thing left in the safe, and she just tossed it into her bag as an after-thought," Viv suggested.

"Maybe she was concerned about it acciden-tally going off in her apartment," Dino said.

"So she transferred the risk to my house?" Stone asked. "I consider that a hostile act."

"Don't be so touchy," Dino said. "We're just brainstorming here."

"Using whose brain?" Stone asked. "Seems to me, we're missing one."

"Now **that's** hostile," Dino said.

"Easy, fellas," Viv said, holding out a calming hand. "We're not getting anywhere."

"Seems to me," Stone said, "that we have arrived at our destination—the only one that makes any sense."

"You have a point," Viv said. "Why don't we wait until you've tried out this theory on Lance, who, as far as I'm concerned, is still a candidate for the bad guy."

A good suggestion. "I'll start trying him as we approach Fort Jefferson."

Stone took out his cell phone, selected the Sonos app, and Oscar Peterson could be heard playing the piano on tiny speakers all around them.

"That's what we need," Viv said. "Soothing music."

STONE WOKE AT dawn, as the engines were starting, then went directly back to sleep. He woke again at mid-morning and looked out a porthole. They were motoring into the harbor at Fort Jefferson, and there was a Coast Guard cutter at anchor there. He got dressed, went on deck, and found Dino and Viv at the rail, looking at the cutter.

"Look who's on deck," Viv said without pointing.

Stone looked and sighted Lance Cabot getting into a rubber dinghy and coming toward where they were mooring.

"Why are you surprised?" Dino asked. "Lance does this sort of thing two or three times a week."

Lance climbed the boarding stairs and set a foot on **Breeze**'s deck. "Is breakfast ready?" he asked.

As it happened, breakfast was, indeed, ready, and they all sat down.

"Before you ask," Lance said. "I arrived in Key West and slept at Stone's house, blissfully without company. I then took the seaplane from Key West International Airport and arrived here an hour ago and was met by the cutter, just in case of unforeseeable problems of any sort."

"Okay," Stone said, "are you ready to be grilled?"

"I perceive that this must be about Vanessa's ready kit," Lance said. "I had her apartment visited yesterday, and it was missing, so . . ."

48

LANCE LOOKED AROUND HIM. "Do I detect a whiff of disbelief?"

"Maybe just a whiff," Stone said. "Why did Vanessa have half a pound of plastique in her go bag?"

Lance shrugged. "Beats me," he said.

"Beats you?" Stone asked. "You're the guy who's supposed to know **everything**!"

"Well, **almost** everything. A committee sits and rules on requests for things like mortars, .50-caliber machine guns, and high explosives. I'd have to go through the records and find out who made the request, what the serial number is, and when it was issued."

Stone reached into the bag and produced the

bomb. "Here you go. We did our best to disarm it, but who knows?"

Lance looked at the device as if it were a poisonous reptile about to strike. "Open it, please."

"Your turn," Stone said. "So far, we've been having all the fun."

Lance got a well-manicured fingernail under one edge and flipped it open. "Ah," he said with a sigh. "Disabled. Good job." He made a phone call and gave somebody a number. "They're checking."

Stone looked at Dino and Viv, who both seemed intensely interested in Lance's conversation.

Lance hung up. "Vanessa didn't requisition it. Jack Collins did."

"For what purpose?" Stone asked.

"I'm afraid that information is above your pay grade," Lance replied regretfully.

Stone waved a hand. "We're all cleared to the same level you are," he said.

"Not quite," Lance replied. "There is a teeny level above you that is reserved for things like high explosives and who receives them in the mail—that sort of thing."

"You mail that stuff?"

"Well, we wouldn't mail it to a residence or even a neighborhood."

"What's left?" Dino asked.

"Oh, things like drug factories and machine shops that manufacture illegal weapons."

"So what was Jack's target when he requisitioned half a pound of plastique?"

Lance gave them another shrug. "Conceivably . . ."

"Actually," Stone said.

"For that information I would have to see the minutes of the meeting in question."

"And you don't have those on you?"

Lance patted his pockets, like a man who had forgotten his wallet when the check arrived. He held up a notebook. "Actually, I do."

"We anxiously await," Stone said.

Lance flipped through his notebook and picked out a scribble with a forefinger. "He requisitioned the explosive for use in the termination, with extreme prejudice, of one Valery Majorov."

Dino spoke up. "So how'd he miss?"

"One is not always successful in these matters."

"By 'one,' you mean Jack? Or just CIA officers in general?" Viv asked.

"In this case, Jack," Lance said. "Though it pains me to tell you. Jack had always been successful in the past."

"So," Viv said, "what you're telling us is, nobody's perfect."

"Well, not Jack, anyway. On this occasion."

"What about the other stuff in the bag?"

"Everybody who leaves the Farm, having performed satisfactorily, is given a sort of tool kit, the contents of which are tailored to the milieu in which the officer will serve."

"What's in this tool kit that wasn't in Jack's?"

"It's hard to say. Jack may have used some of his tools, then discarded them. Absent finger-prints and DNA, of course."

"Of course," Stone said. "Now, what do we do with half a pound of military-grade plastique?"

"Well," Lance said, "it's a bit rich for a fire-works display, isn't it?"

"I suppose so."

"Perhaps if you just hold on to the substance for a while, a suitable opportunity will present itself."

"I don't really trust myself with this sort of thing," Stone said. "Do you know who I trust with it?"

"Who would that be?"

"You," Stone said, pushing the disabled bomb across the table.

Lance looked at it for a moment, checked the wiring again, then slipped it into a jacket pocket. "There," he said. "All secure."

"And if it turns out not to be," Stone said, "I expect we'll hear about it."

49

THEY FINISHED THEIR BREAKFAST. "Lance?" Stone said.

Lance dabbed at his chin with the linen napkin. "Yes?"

"Do you think we could lose the Coast Guard cutter?"

"It's very good protection," Lance said, "and they went to a good deal of trouble to get in here."

"No more trouble than we went to," Stone pointed out. "Also, it's as though the cutter were waving a big banner reading VERY IMPORTANT PERSON ABOARD THE ADJACENT YACHT. Part of the trouble we went to getting here was remaining unnoticed."

Lance sighed. "The cutter was in the neighborhood," he said.

"Funny, our crew didn't spot it until we found it present on our arrival."

Lance made a phone call. "Captain? Lance Cabot. We are feeling secure, now, and no longer require your assistance. Yes, and thank you so much!" He hung up. "There," he said.

Immediately the noise of the cutter's anchor coming up was heard, and shortly it passed out of the lagoon and away from the fort.

"Where's it going?" Stone asked.

"Wherever it likes," Lance replied. "It's a big ocean."

"I sort of liked having it here," Viv said. "It was comforting, somehow."

"I thought we all agreed that it would attract too much attention," Stone said.

"Well, yes, but . . ."

"It's gone, Viv," Stone said. "Get over it."

"I'll try."

"What'll we do until lunch?" Dino asked.

"Board games, yesterday's **Times,** or jumping into the water and flapping your arms to attract sharks," Stone suggested.

"Can we hit some golf balls?" Dino asked.

"Not unless we want to cover the lagoon bottom with old golf balls, many of them with my name stamped on them."

"You don't mind that at golf courses," Dino pointed out.

"There they have men with Aqua-Lungs who

swim around the bottom, retrieving them and selling them back to me."

"How about shooting skeet?"

"Too noisy."

"How about shooting Dino?" Viv asked. "Only the first round will be noisy."

"Dino," Stone said, "boredom is a self-inflicted wound. Heal thyself."

Dino got up, went below, and returned in a swimsuit. He vaulted over the rail and made a big splash.

"Great," Viv said, "now all I need is a speargun."

She went below, changed, and came back looking very good in a small bikini. She jumped in with Dino.

Stone began to miss Vanessa all over again.

STONE FINISHED THE crossword and lay back on the afterdeck cushions for a nap. After what seemed only a moment, he heard distant thunder. He jerked awake and sat up, looking around.

"It's only the tourist seaplane from Key West to Fort Jefferson," Lance said. "Relax."

Stone got out his iPhone and turned on some Oscar Peterson.

"That beats an aircraft engine every time," Lance said.

Stone, who was unaccustomed to hearing Lance

express such an opinion, sat up and looked around. "It stopped," he said.

"It's at the dock, disgorging passengers for a thirty-minute walk around the fort." Lance put down the book he had been reading. "I think I'll return to Key West with them."

"As you wish," Stone said, buzzing the skipper and asking for a dinghy and crew for the short ride in. Stone napped again, then a few minutes later, he awoke to the sound of the seaplane lifting off and flying away.

Lance was gone. The plastique bomb was lying on the coffee table.

50

Stone slept badly and awoke breathing heavily, sweating, and hearing distant thunder. He sat up and shook his head, yawned, sang a few bars of "Daisy Bell," moved all his fingers and toes, sure that he had had a stroke. His vision tilted about thirty degrees. He wondered why everything on deck didn't slide into the sea. He blinked furiously. After nearly a minute of this, he heard a woman's voice: "Good morning, Stone."

Then everything snapped back into place. Vanessa was sitting across from him at the table in a comfortable chair, almost dressed in a bikini.

"Not you," Stone managed to say.

"Aren't you glad to see me?" she asked.

He fell back onto the sofa, unconscious.

———

SOMEONE WAS SHAKING him, then harder.

"Stone? Wake up!" It was Dino's voice.

He opened an eye. Viv was patting his face with a towel. "What's wrong, Stone?" she asked. "You're soaking wet!"

He sat up and looked around. "Where is she?"

"Who?" Dino asked.

"Vanessa. She was just here."

"Listen, pal. You snap out of it, or I'm going to have to throw you overboard to wake you up!"

"You were making terrible noises," Viv said.

"Did you hear the thunder?" he asked.

Dino picked up an icy drink on the coffee table and threw the contents into Stone's face.

"What was that?" Stone asked.

"A gin and tonic. I made it for you earlier."

"What was in it?"

"Well, let's see," Dino said, scratching his head, "there was gin, and there was tonic."

"Don't be a smart-ass! What else was in it?"

"Oh, I remember," Dino said, "a wedge of lime."

"Where is it?"

Dino looked around and picked up something from the sofa, next to Stone. "Look, a wedge of lime." He made to suck it, but Stone grabbed his wrist. "No. I want it analyzed."

"Well," Dino said, "I don't have my lime juice

analysis kit on me, so we'll just have to wait until we get back to New York." He popped the lime wedge into his shirt pocket.

"Don't lose it. It's important. Where's Vanessa?"

"Still on a slab in the New York City morgue, I expect," Dino said.

"No, she's aboard."

"Where?" Dino asked, looking around.

Viv was just peering into Stone's face, without speaking.

"I think maybe you should lie back down for a while," Dino said.

"I don't want to. I want to see Vanessa. She has some explaining to do."

"I don't know what she could possibly tell us," Dino said. "Are you looking for a message from the other side?"

"The other side of the coffee table," Stone said, pointing at the empty chair. "She was sitting right there, in a bikini, almost."

"Almost what?" Dino asked.

"I know what he means," Viv said. "He's not crazy, and he hasn't had a stroke." She reached into Dino's shirt pocket and extracted the lime. She squeezed it slightly, then put it to her nose. "Amyl nitrate," she said. "Or that's my best guess, anyway. It's been a long time."

Dino smelled the lime. "Jesus, I think you're right," he said.

"You slipped me a mickey," Stone said.

"No, somebody slipped me the mickey, and I unknowingly passed it on."

"What were you drinking?" Stone asked.

"Scotch on the rocks," they both said.

"No lime?"

"On Scotch? Are you kidding me?"

"It's gone," Stone said, pointing at the coffee table.

"The lime?" Dino asked. "Viv has it."

Stone pointed at the table and shook his finger at it. "No, not the lime, the . . . other thing." For the life of him, he couldn't remember the word. Shaking his finger at the table wasn't helping, but he continued to do it.

"The other thing?" Viv asked.

"What other thing?" Dino followed.

"The goddamned other thing that was there!"

"Stone, you're babbling. Lie down again," Dino said.

"I don't want to lie down!"

And then they heard a faint noise from the cabin below.

"What was that?" Stone asked.

"A toilet flushing," Viv said.

"Must be the maid," Dino offered.

"Too early," Stone said. "They don't start before noon, in case we're sleeping in."

"I know what's missing," Viv said.

"What is it?" Dino demanded.

"The plastique bomb," she said.

And then there was the sound of flip-flops from the companionway stairs, and Vanessa stepped onto the deck.

51

EVERYBODY STOOD, FROZEN, saying nothing. Finally, Dino spoke. "Okay, Stone," he said, "you're not crazy. **I'm** crazy."

"Me, too," Viv said.

And then the apparition spoke. "Nobody's crazy. I'm not dead."

"Prove it," Dino said.

"What do you want me to do? Bleed for you?"

"Don't bother," Stone said. "You've convinced me. Please sit down so I don't have to look up at you."

Vanessa sat down and crossed her legs. "Well?"

"Explain yourself," Stone said. "And don't leave anything out."

"Dino made a mistake," she said. "He found the wrong corpse."

"You think I never examined a corpse?" Dino asked, his voice rising.

"I didn't say that," Vanessa replied. "I said you examined the **wrong** corpse. It was understandable, being covered in blood and all that. I found it about thirty seconds before you did. When you and Stone went out to the vestibule with guns drawn, I grabbed my little bag, then ran through the kitchen and out to the service elevator. I rode it to the basement, then ran into the alley and up to the street, where I got a cab."

"Why didn't you say something to somebody?" Stone asked.

"Because I didn't want to be surrounded by cops and, maybe, arrested for murder. I knew where you were heading, since I was meant to go with you. I went to LaGuardia and got a nonstop to Key West. I remembered that you lived next to a strip joint called Bare Assets, so I went there and looked up the street beside it. I found your name on the mailbox. I went in, and a housekeeper said you had just called and were taking a cruise instead."

"Sane, so far," Stone admitted.

"Then Lance walked in. I surprised him, too. After he calmed down, we had a conversation about where you had gone, and he made some phone calls and said you wouldn't get where you were going until the next day. So yesterday we took the little seaplane out here, where we were met by the Coast Guard cutter, and we were aboard that until you arrived."

"How'd you get aboard without being seen?"

"Did you see Lance come aboard?"

"Well, no."

"He's sneaky that way. He put me in an empty cabin up forward, told me to wait until some things were settled, and eventually, I came up here."

"Who was the dead woman in your bathroom?" Dino asked.

"I don't know."

"I can guess," Stone said.

"So, guess," Dino replied.

"Remember the lovely Anna?"

"She was never caught. She could have been anywhere. Why would she go after Vanessa?" Dino said.

"To keep her from ratting out Majorov."

"Oh, shit. Well, at least we don't have to worry about her anymore."

"There was somebody else in my apartment that I didn't know about," Vanessa said. "I think he killed her, then got out the same way I did, but earlier." She recrossed her legs. "I think that about covers it," she said.

"And it was you who put the amyl nitrate in my lime?"

"It was not," she replied firmly. "Who else was here?"

"Lance," Stone said. "But why would he want to do that?"

"Beats me, but I saw him do it. Maybe he just wanted to confuse you."

"Well, that worked," Stone replied. "I thought I had had a stroke."

"No," Viv said. "The amyl nitrate covers all your symptoms—at least, one squirt would. Two squirts of lime juice, and you'd have just passed out for a while."

"Where's the plastique bomb?" Stone asked.

"I flushed it down the toilet at the bottom of the stairs."

"That didn't clog it?"

"Nope, it went straight down and out to wherever things go."

"No," Stone said. "We can't flush into these waters. It went into the holding tank. Has anybody pooped since we got aboard?"

All heads were shaken.

Stone picked up a phone and asked Todd to inspect the tank and to bring in any unusual object he found there.

"Why do you want the thing?" Dino asked.

"Because I don't want it to accidentally go off in the holding tank. I don't know how I would explain it to my partners in the yacht. I don't think our insurance covers that."

"Better safe than sorry," Vanessa said.

"You should have thought of that before you flushed," Stone replied.

52

THEY ATE LUNCH pretty much in silence. When they had finished, Dino said, "Why are you so quiet, Stone?"

"I'm figuring out who's going to try to kill us next."

"Valery Majorov," Dino said. "Who's left?"

"Okay, it's Majorov. How's he going to try to do it?"

"Well, the bomb is tucked away somewhere below," Dino said. "In the maid's closet in the hallway."

"Means of attempt on us: sniper?"

"From where? We've got pretty much a 360-degree view from the yacht, and I can't see a sniper's perch from where I'm sitting."

"You see my dilemma," Stone said.

"How about an air attack?" Dino said.

"The only airplane hereabouts is the tourists' seaplane from Key West, and I don't think that's equipped for strafing or bombing."

As if on cue, there was a buzzing from the sky. Stone grabbed a handheld radio and raised Captain Todd. "You've got some rifles aboard, haven't you?"

"Yep, two of them."

"Load them and bring them on deck, will you."

"Yes, sir. You want the shotguns we use for skeet?"

"If you've got any buckshot."

"I'll check."

Stone got up and peered out from under the deck awning toward the east. "It's coming."

The skipper arrived on deck with an armful of long guns and some boxes of ammo.

"Dino," Stone said, "get the ladies to loading and you go below and bring up our handguns."

"Mine, too," Vanessa said. "It's in my ready bag."

"Stone," Dino said, "even if we get lucky, I don't know if we can get away with shooting down a planeload of tourists."

"Just get the handguns. If they know we're armed, that might hold them off."

Dino went below.

The airplane lined up into the wind, set down in the lagoon, and taxied to the dock at the fort.

Dino came up from below and deposited three handguns on the dining table.

Passengers began to leave the airplane and walk to the fort. Soon it was empty.

"Well," Viv said, "that was a pretty good drill."

"The next one might not be a drill," Stone said.

"Well, we've got an hour or two before it comes back with another load. Time to build a fort on the upper deck." She and Vanessa laughed a lot.

"I'm happy to have weapons at hand, anyway," Dino said. "There's something comforting about live ammo."

"Let's go upstairs and have a look around." Stone grabbed two rifles and handed Dino one. The women took the remaining shotguns. "There's no buckshot," Viv said, "but we can make noise, I guess."

Stone's phone rang. "Yes?"

"It's Lance."

"You miserable son of a bitch!" Stone shouted into the instrument. "You poisoned my lime!"

"Nonsense," Lance replied. "You were all worked up, and I thought you might do something crazy, so I gave you a little sedative."

"You think I was worked up then, you should see me now, when I'm armed!"

"There's nothing to shoot at out there except the tourist seaplane. Now, don't you go taking potshots at that thing!"

"If you show up here again, I'll be shooting at you!" Stone shouted, then hung up.

"I don't think Lance is accustomed to being shouted at," Vanessa said, "let alone to being shot at."

"Well, he'd better get used to it," Stone said.

"Stone," Viv said. "Can I get you a gin and tonic?"

"That's not funny!"

"Yes, it is," Dino said, shaking with laughter.

"If you're going to shake, put down that weapon!" Stone said.

Dino set his rifle on the table with the other weapons. "Sure thing, pal. I wouldn't want you to shoot me."

The phone rang again and Stone answered it. "You again?"

"I had hoped you might have cooled down a bit by now," Lance said.

"Well, you can hope." Stone hung up again.

Dino opened the upper-deck bar cabinet. "How about a Knob Creek. With no lime?" He put some ice in a glass and poured one.

"Sold," Stone said, reaching for the drink.

53

STONE'S PHONE RANG AGAIN.

"Lance?" Dino asked.

"Yes." Stone picked up the phone. "Now what?"

"Calm down, Stone," Lance said soothingly. "Anger is self-destructive."

"Well, I'm looking for somebody else to destroy," Stone said. "Have you got any suggestions as to who or how we're going to be attacked?"

"Well, you're pretty exposed out there. You could take the tourist plane back, I guess. No, wait. It's always fully booked."

"Anything else?"

"A moving target is harder to hit. Why don't you weigh anchor and get the hell out of there?"

"Finally, a sensible suggestion from somebody! Captain!" Stone shouted into the intercom.

"Weigh anchor and sail for Key West and the sub base! Warp speed!"

"Yes, sir!" Engines were started, and a grinding noise signaled the anchor coming up. They moved toward the channel and sailed around the fort, then headed east.

"Let's get back to the main deck," Stone said, gathering up a couple of the rifles. "We're too noticeable up here."

They all clambered down the stairs and disported themselves around the fantail. Vanessa stripped off her bikini top, and Viv got Dino with a backhand when he turned to look at the half-naked woman. Stone enjoyed the view.

Captain Todd came to them. "We're making fifteen knots through the water," he said, "but we're using a hell of a lot of fuel. Shall we bear the expense?"

"Damn the torpedoes and the expenses," Stone said, "full speed ahead!"

"I think we've got enough fuel to make the sub base," the skipper said.

"Think?" Stone said. "I think we'd better **know**! There's no fuel between here and Key West."

"Okay, I know," Todd said. "We'll have an hour's fuel when we get there."

"You'd better arrange for the oiler to meet us at the sub base, in case we have to run for it again."

"Done." The skipper beat a retreat before Stone could think of other orders.

"This is just wonderful," Vanessa said, leaning back to get the most sun. Stone was hoping she'd take off the bikini bottom, too, but he didn't want to rile Viv further by asking her to.

"Wonderful," Vanessa said again.

Stone scanned the horizon behind them. "Wonderful, except for **that**," he said, nodding at a black dot behind them on the horizon. "Distant thunder."

"What?" Dino asked. "I don't see anything."

"Let's hope it doesn't get any bigger," Stone said. Fifteen minutes later, it was bigger.

"I see it," Dino said. "How fast do you think he's going?"

"Faster than we are," Stone said. "Let's hope she's burning fuel as fast as we are, too."

They watched the dot grow larger, then, an hour later, become, identifiably, a boat.

"Looks like a trawler of some kind," Dino said, holding up a pair of the yacht's binoculars.

"Let's hope so. Trawlers aren't all that fast," Stone replied.

The boat grew larger. "Dino," Stone said, "please go below and get the bomb, and bring it and all its pieces up here."

"Do you know how to put it together?" Dino asked.

"No, but Vanessa does."

Vanessa opened an eye. "Did I hear my name mentioned?"

"Yes. Dino has gone to get the bomb. It will be your job to get it in working order, and pretty quick, too. In the meantime, we'll use you for distraction."

"Okay. You want me to take my bottoms off, too?"

"Sure," Stone replied offhandedly, "why not?"

Viv seemed to have dozed off. Dino would be glad.

Dino made the main deck again and tiptoed to the fantail, holding a paper shopping bag by the handles. Viv dozed on.

"I'm going to need a towel and some tools," Vanessa said. "The tools are in my ready bag."

"Dino?" Stone said. "Ready bag?" He tossed Vanessa the smallest towel he could find, and she spread it over her lap and shook out the contents of the paper bag onto it.

Dino returned with the ready kit and handed it to her, obviously disappointed with the location of the towel.

"Now, let's see," Vanessa said. "How does this go?"

Stone winced. Dino looked horrified.

54

THE SKIPPER GOT another knot or two out of **Breeze,** and the trawler seemed not to be gaining anymore. Stone reckoned they were a mile or so back. He wondered how running full out was going to affect **Breeze**'s engines.

Vanessa was using the binoculars. "I see a man."

"Do you recognize him?" Stone asked.

"He could be Majorov, but I've only seen him once before, so I can't be sure."

Stone used the binoculars, but the man was now obscured by the wheelhouse of the trawler. The skipper called on the handheld. "How are we doing? Are they gaining on us?"

"We seem to be holding our lead," Stone replied. "How are our engines doing?"

"We're running at full revs, and I don't like

doing that, but they're new enough that they might take it without blowing up."

"Temperatures?" Stone asked.

"Just inside the green line. We don't want to go into the red."

"Right." Stone put the radio down and checked the trawler's position again.

Dino picked up one of the rifles. "You want me to take a shot at them? It might discourage them."

"That's a Winchester model 1873 replica," Stone said. "I don't think we could do anything to them at this range, in a moving boat, and we might just make them angry."

"They look pretty angry already," Dino said. "One other thing, they might have a weapon that's higher powered than ours, and I don't think this is a good time to find out. How long till port?"

"I don't know. A couple of hours to the harbor, I guess, then we have to slow down on the way to the sub base."

"Should we call the Coast Guard?"

"And tell them what? That we're being pursued by an angry lobsterman? I don't think that would bring them, guns ablaze."

Dino leaned in. "If they could see Vanessa, **that** would bring them."

Stone looked at Vanessa, lying on her back, asleep, her breasts rolling a little with the sea.

Stone's phone rang. Lance. "Yes?"

"You're holding your own," Lance said. "Keep it up."

"We're trying. Have you got us on satellite?"

"Yes, our camera seems to be about fifty feet above you. Vanessa looks very nice. There's been a parade of people through here, checking her out. She's not going to have any tan lines, is she?"

"Can you see any armaments on the trawler, or is Vanessa blocking the view?"

"Nothing as yet. I'll call you if we see any sign of hostile intent." Lance hung up.

"What does Lance have to say for himself?" Dino asked.

"Nothing, but a lot about Vanessa. Did she finish the bomb?"

"I guess. How are you planning to use it?"

"Just to scare them off," Stone said. "If necessary."

A crewman served them some chilled gazpacho, in mugs. Viv threw a towel over Vanessa, and the crewman departed, looking disappointed. Vanessa had to be awakened to take her soup.

BEFORE VANESSA COULD go back to sleep, Stone asked her about the bomb. "Well, I think it's all hooked up," she said, opening the shopping bag and holding it up.

Stone winced. "How do we set it off?"

"The cell phone's already been disconnected: I figure if you use it, you'll be throwing it, so all you do is press this button," she said, pointing at it, "and you've got ten seconds to get rid of it, before it goes off."

Stone's mouth went dry, and he lubricated it with a swig of Bloody Mary.

Dino stood up and pointed. "I think that must be Key West," he said.

Stone looked at the lump on the horizon and nodded. "About half an hour to the channel, another fifteen or twenty minutes to the sub base."

"Ask Vanessa if I can hold her towel for her," Dino suggested.

"Sit down and shut up," Stone said, "or your wife will emasculate you."

That had the desired effect.

55

Dino tapped Stone on the shoulder and pointed toward the pass through the reef to the harbor. "Is that going to be a problem?"

Stone followed his finger and his eyes came to an abrupt halt. "Holy shit," he said. Dino's finger was pointing at a gigantic cruise ship entering Key West Harbor. "How did that thing sneak up on us?"

"I was wondering that, too."

"It's headed for the ship dock over there, right next to the channel," Stone said, "so it will be slowing down to a crawl as it moseys up to the dock."

"What's that boat alongside her?"

"I think that's a harbor vessel assigned to see

that nobody gets too close to her on the sea-ward side."

"Like us?"

"Yep."

"And like the trawler behind us, too?"

"Yep. It occurs to me that they're not going to want five hundred witnesses hanging over the rail of the ship, gawking at us both." He pointed at the five hundred witnesses.

"So they'll wait until we're at the sub pen be-fore they make their move?"

"Yeah, and it's our only move. It's too shallow to our left and there's a big marina to the right of the channel. It's the sub base or just stop dead in the water, in what you might call the 'sitting duck' position."

"And how is that going to differ from our posi-tion at the sub dock?"

"Not much," Stone replied.

"That's what I thought."

"Why don't you and I each take a Winchester up to the top deck, keeping low. Maybe we can make it without the folks on the trawler seeing us."

"Couldn't hurt," Dino replied, handing Stone a rifle and grabbing a box of ammunition.

As an afterthought, Stone grabbed the shop-ping bag holding the bomb.

"After you," Dino said.

Stone crouched and ran along the deck to the stairs, then ran up them and hid behind a big Boston whaler the crew used for shopping ashore. He sat down and leaned against the boat and watched Dino coming his way.

"What are we going to do about the harbor boat protecting the cruise ship?" Dino asked.

"We're going to trust the skipper not to hit it."

"Good idea."

Stone popped up for a quick look around. "One hundred yards to the channel," he said. "The trawler is going to overtake us soon."

"Are we going to fire first?"

"Are you kidding, Dino? There might be a troop of Girl Scouts aboard that boat—we don't know, do we?"

"I guess not."

"Then we'll hold our fire, until they're not holding theirs anymore."

"I hope they're bad shots," Dino said.

"Jesus, the girls are on the main deck and exposed."

"Nah, they headed below with the handguns as soon as we came up here."

"So Vanessa is no longer a distraction?"

"No, I'm sorry to say. I was enjoying being distracted."

"I think you can be sure that Viv is getting Vanessa dressed as we speak."

"It's just the sort of thing she'd do," Dino said sorrowfully.

"I don't know what your current standing with the Catholic church is," Stone said, "but this would be a good time to pray."

Dino crossed himself. "Let's see if anybody's listening," he said, moving his lips silently.

Something struck the whaler and shook it.

"Too late," Stone said.

56

STONE POPPED HIS HEAD up and had a look to port, then drew back, but not before inviting several rounds to be fired at the whaler. "Their rounds are not penetrating," Stone said. "There's a layer of Kevlar in the hull."

"Good for us."

"Yes, but we can't see anything. Let's get aboard the whaler."

"You first," Dino replied.

Stone half stood, then drew back a leg and threw it over the side of the whaler, like a cowboy mounting a horse, and got into the boat.

Dino did the same.

Stone's phone rang. "Yes?"

"That's a good spot for you," Lance said. "The hull of that boat is very tough."

"I figured that out," Stone said. "Do you have anything new for us?"

"As a matter of fact, I do. The trawler seems to have used its engine a little too hard. There's smoke trailing from the on-deck engine cover. And they've slowed more than they needed to, while they try to figure out what's wrong. They're still a hundred yards behind you and moving very slowly."

Stone popped up to look ahead of them and didn't draw fire. "Our berth is fifty yards away, and the skipper is creeping up on it."

"Why haven't you been shot in the head?" Dino asked.

"Because something's wrong aboard the trawler. Lance says they're trailing smoke from the engine cover on deck." He looked aft, and so did Dino.

Dino fired a couple of rounds from his Winchester into the deck, and three or four men on the trawler took cover. "That ought to slow them down with the repairs," he said.

Breeze was in her berth now, and shore hands were securing her warps. Stone looked back and saw the trawler, maybe fifty yards back. A man in the wheelhouse was moving back and forth, pulling levers and pressing buttons.

"They'll have an automatic fire extinguisher in the engine bay," Stone said.

"Then why aren't they using it?" Dino asked.

"Maybe it went off, but it didn't do the job." Two men ran from cover and tried to open the engine cover but failed.

Dino drove them away from the engine cover with a couple of well-placed rounds. A man came out of the wheelhouse holding a sinister-looking rifle with a scope and a silencer and held it to his shoulder.

Dino racked his Winchester and shot him, knocking him backward onto the deck of the trawler.

"Good shot, Dino!" Stone yelled, firing a couple of rounds with his own weapon. "That ought to keep their heads down."

The shooter aboard the trawler struggled to his feet and rested the barrel of his rifle on the wheelhouse. Dino put a round into the wooden railing next to him, and he ducked. "I think we have an advantage in height here," Dino said.

Then, from the trawler, came the roar of the engine, and even more smoke poured out of the hatch, which the crew had finally torn off.

Dino and Stone emptied their weapons into the cockpit of the trawler.

Stone looked around. "Where's the ammo?"

"Oh, shit, I left it on the upper deck when we climbed into the whaler."

"Well, we're both out," Stone said. "Does that give you any ideas?"

Dino jumped over the side of the whaler,

retrieved the bag holding the ammunition, and tossed it into the whaler, then jumped back in. He opened a box of cartridges, and they both started loading them into the Winchesters' magazines. The windshield on the whaler exploded, showering them with glass fragments.

"I guess they forgot to make that bulletproof, huh?" Dino said.

Stone looked up again, and the trawler was on the move once more. "Stand by to repel boarders!" he said.

The trawler was twenty-five yards out and aiming to come alongside **Breeze.**

Stone and Dino fired more rounds into the trawler's cockpit and into the wheelhouse windshield, which crazed but didn't shatter.

The trawler, amazingly, hadn't slowed and was making a good five knots toward the yacht.

"Shit," Stone said, "they don't have any control of the power. They're going to ram us. Brace for it!" They held on to whatever they could find.

57

The TRAWLER HAD STOPPED, but it was a good four or five feet from the yacht. Engine-starting noises were coming from the craft.

Dino was pouring rounds into the wheelhouse and the deck, and when he ran out, he grabbed Stone's rifle and began firing his rounds, too.

Stone heard the trawler's engine restart, and the boat began to move forward.

"He's having steering problems!" Dino shouted.

In desperation, Stone grabbed the shopping bag, opened the flap on the bomb, and pressed the button. "Ten, nine, eight, seven . . ." he counted. Then he stood up, grabbed the handles of the shopping bag, swung his arm, and tossed the bag, underhand, at the boat. There was too much smoke coming out of the engine bay to see where the bomb had landed, or even if it had hit the boat.

"Let's get out of here!" Stone shouted, vaulting over the whaler's rail and onto **Breeze**'s upper deck. "Four seconds left."

Dino was gathering both rifles and the ammo bag and tossing them at Stone.

"Get out of there, Dino!" Stone shouted. "Two seconds!"

Dino landed near Stone, and they both ran across the upper deck and threw themselves, facedown, onto the teak, covering their heads as best they could.

Nothing happened.

"What the hell?" Stone yelled at Dino. "It didn't go off!"

"How should I know?" Dino yelled back. "Vanessa and you armed the thing!"

"I pressed the button, and it was supposed to give us ten seconds."

"Maybe you threw long, and it went overboard." Dino pointed. "Look!"

Stone sat up and saw the trawler's stern as it passed **Breeze**'s bow. "It's still underway, and with no steerage!"

The two of them struggled to their feet and looked down the channel.

"I don't understand," Stone said.

Then he understood. The trawler exploded, apparently from the inside.

"Thar she blows!" Stone shouted.

"She do," Dino agreed.

Then she blew again.

"Fuel tank," Stone said.

"Diesel doesn't explode like that," Dino said. "They must have a gasoline engine."

"And they're welcome to it," Stone said.

They heard a siren and turned to look aft. A Coast Guard rigid rubber dinghy of about thirty feet was backing out of the sub base and into the channel. A moment later, they were passing **Breeze,** headed toward the remains of the trawler, which were partly afloat but surrounded by debris and what looked like bodies, or parts of them.

"What the hell was that?" Viv yelled.

Stone turned and saw her coming up the stairs to the top deck, followed closely by Vanessa.

"That was Vanessa's bomb going off on the trawler, followed by a gasoline explosion."

Vanessa gave Stone a big kiss. "Did you throw the bomb at them?"

"Yes, and I think it went down the open engine hatch," Stone said.

"I'm glad I gave you the extra time," she said.

"What extra time?"

"I reset it to give you thirty seconds, just in case."

"Ah, that would explain why Stone and I are still alive!" Dino crowed.

"Excuse me, people," Stone said, "but I think we're going to have a visit from the Coast Guard very soon. So we should put the yacht in order."

"What order?" Viv asked.

"Well, you could start by getting those handguns below," he said, "and well-hidden. Vanessa, that evil bag of yours needs to disappear, too, along with anything inside it or outside it that might be bomb-related. When they come aboard, please let me do all the talking, so we won't contradict ourselves. Just make positive noises now and then."

"Okay, pal," Dino said. "You can screw this up all by yourself."

58

THEY WERE GATHERED around the dining table aboard **Breeze,** and as far as Stone could tell, there were present a crusty, fiftyish Coast Guard captain, a young woman who was skipper of the cutter, a couple of Key West police detectives, and two men and a woman in civilian clothes, who could be FBI or some other agency.

Ahead of them, in the channel that ran past the sub base, was a smoldering pile of floating debris that had once been a trawler. All this created a clog in the channel, and there were angry boaters lined up at both ends, waiting to get wherever they were going.

The Coast Guard captain took charge. "All right," he said, "what the hell happened here?"

Stone raised a finger. "Perhaps I can help."

"Are you the owner of this yacht?"

"I am one of three partners in her ownership."

"Go on."

"We were anchored out at the fort, and I received a call warning that there might be a vessel in the neighborhood that meant us harm, so at daylight we weighed anchor and sailed for, well, right here. Later in the morning we spotted a vessel far in our wake that seemed to be following us."

"How far in your wake?"

Stone took him through the sequence of events, skipping the part about the bomb he had thrown.

"And you exchanged small-arms fire with the trawler as it approached you?"

"We **returned** small-arms fire, in fear of our lives. They seemed to have us outgunned."

"What made the trawler explode?"

"I believe it may have been propelled by a gasoline engine, and as the trawler passed us, there seemed to be a fire belowdecks, perhaps in the engine room."

"That would account for one explosion," the captain said.

"Perhaps they had two engines, or just two fuel tanks," Stone offered.

"Did you know anyone aboard the trawler?"

"I didn't see any familiar faces," Stone replied. Someone came on deck behind Stone and approached the table. "Perhaps I can be of assistance," Lance Cabot said. He handed the captain his card and sat down.

"Ladies and gentlemen," the captain said, in a voice dripping with sarcasm. "We have the honor to be in the august presence of the director of Central Intelligence."

"The honor is mine," Lance replied, absent the sarcasm.

"Enlighten us, Director Cabot," the captain said.

"Those aboard the trawler had been identified by one of our officers as members of a gang of Russian criminals, who held a grudge against one or more of those sailing aboard **Breeze**."

"Which ones?" the captain demanded.

"I'm very much afraid that I must invoke national security in not replying to your question. The answer is not relevant to our discussion, in any case. Suffice it to say that they were being hunted as prey by evil men, and the actions taken aboard this yacht were entirely in response to those initiated aboard the trawler. It would seem that in their chase of the yacht they overtaxed their engines and started a fire on board." Lance handed the captain a large brown envelope. "This was taken about half an hour before the resulting explosions. Note the smoke streaming from the engine bay."

The captain removed a photograph from the envelope, looked at it, then passed it around the table. "You were flying over the scene, were you?"

"Not exactly," Lance replied. "That photograph was produced by means that I cannot identify—once again, for reasons of national security. You have my assurance that it has been in no way doctored, except to be enlarged."

"So you take it that no one aboard the yacht had any part in starting that fire?"

"I do. At the time it was taken, which is stamped in a corner, shots had not yet been fired from either vessel, so their engine fire was entirely self-generated."

The captain seemed somewhat deflated, as if he had intended to tear into everybody. "Does anyone have any questions?" he asked, looking around the table.

His question was met by silence. Everyone looked anywhere but at him.

"Well, then," the captain said, stuffing the satshot into his briefcase. "I find that no offense was committed by anyone aboard this yacht, and that the offenders, whoever they were, caused the damage to their own vessel and their own deaths." He stood, and everyone stood with him. They filed to the boarding stairs and off the yacht.

Stone emitted a sigh of relief. "Just in time, Lance."

"He did seem upset, didn't he?"

"I think he was looking forward to personally conducting a hanging," Stone replied.

"I enjoy disappointing authority," Lance said, "unless the authority is mine."

"Will you stay aboard for dinner?" Stone asked.

"I will, thank you, and if you're headed back to Teterboro, I would be grateful for a lift."

"I'll order the aircraft for eight o'clock," Stone said.

59

THE GROUP WAS all pretty quiet on the flight home. Vanessa slept, unfortunately, fully clothed. Everyone deplaned, Stone last, because he had to find his briefcase. When Stone came down the stairs he looked around and Vanessa was gone. Lance rode in with Stone because, as it turned out, he was begging a bed as well.

Helene made a late-night nibble and a nightcap for them, and they sat in Stone's study. "Fill in the blanks for me, Lance," Stone said.

"There are no blanks to fill," Lance replied. "You know everything you should know, perhaps even more than you should know."

Stone took a breath to ask a question, but Lance stilled him with a raised hand. "Either you already know the answer to your question, or you should not know. I thought I explained that."

"So I can never ask a question again?"

"Not on the subject of the past few weeks."

"I don't suppose I should ask where Vanessa went, then?"

"Oh, that reminds me," Lance said, patting his pockets and coming up with an envelope. "She asked me to give you this after we got home."

Stone opened the envelope and took out a single sheet of paper. The note was brief:

My dear Stone,
**   I want to thank you for all your kindnesses of the past weeks. I have enjoyed myself immensely.**
**   Now, I fear, I must cease to exist, so we will not speak again.**
Fondly, Vanessa

Stone turned to Lance, who held up a restraining hand. "You either know, or shouldn't," he said.

END
April 8, 2022
Washington, Connecticut

AUTHOR'S NOTE

I am happy to hear from readers, but you should know that if you write to me in care of my publisher, three to six months will pass before I receive your letter, and when it finally arrives it will be one among many, and I will not be able to reply.

However, if you have access to the Internet, you may visit my website at www.stuartwoods .com, where there is a button for sending me e-mail. So far, I have been able to reply to all my e-mail, and I will continue to try to do so.

If you send me an e-mail and do not receive a reply, it is probably because you are among an alarming number of people who have entered their e-mail address incorrectly in their mail software. I have many of my replies returned as undeliverable.

Remember: e-mail, reply; snail mail, no reply.

When you e-mail, please do not send attachments, as I never open those. They can take twenty minutes to download, and they often contain viruses.

Please do not place me on your mailing lists for funny stories, prayers, political causes, charitable fundraising, petitions, or sentimental claptrap. I get enough of that from people I already know. Generally speaking, when I get e-mail addressed to a large number of people, I immediately delete it without reading it.

Please do not send me your ideas for a book, as I have a policy of writing only what I myself invent. If you send me story ideas, I will immediately delete them without reading them. If you have a good idea for a book, write it yourself, but I will not be able to advise you on how to get it published. Buy a copy of **Writer's Market** at any bookstore; that will tell you how.

Anyone with a request concerning events or appearances may e-mail it to me or send it to: Penguin Random House LLC, 1745 Broadway, New York, NY 10019.

Those ambitious folk who wish to buy film, dramatic, or television rights to my books should contact Matthew Snyder, Creative Artists Agency, 2000 Avenue of the Stars, Los Angeles, CA 90067.

Those who wish to make offers for rights of

a literary nature should contact Anne Sibbald, Janklow & Nesbit, 285 Madison Avenue, 21st Floor, New York, NY 10017. (Note: This is not an invitation for you to send her your manuscript or to solicit her to be your agent.)

If you want to know if I will be signing books in your city, please visit my website, www.stuartwoods.com, where the tour schedule will be published a month or so in advance. If you wish me to do a book signing in your locality, ask your favorite bookseller to contact his Penguin Random House representative or the Putnam publicity department with the request.

If you find typographical or editorial errors in my book and feel an irresistible urge to tell someone, please write to Gabriella Mongelli at Penguin's address above. Do not e-mail your discoveries to me, as I will already have learned about them from others.

A list of my published works appears in the front of this book and on my website. All the novels are still in print in paperback and can be found at or ordered from any bookstore. If you wish to obtain hardcover copies of earlier novels or of the two nonfiction books, a good used-book store or one of the online bookstores can help you find them. Otherwise, you will have to go to a great many garage sales.

STUART WOODS was the author of more than ninety novels, including the #1 **New York Times** bestselling Stone Barrington series. A native of Georgia and an avid sailor and pilot, he began his writing career in the advertising industry. **Chiefs,** his debut in 1981, won the Edgar Award. Woods passed away in 2022.

LIKE WHAT YOU'VE READ?

Try these titles by Stuart Woods,
also available in large print:

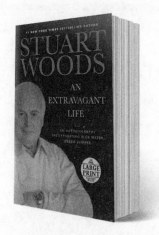

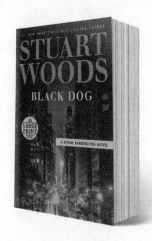

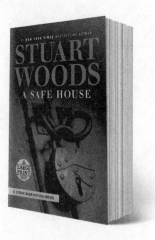

An Extravagant Life
ISBN 978-0-593-60762-6

Black Dog
ISBN 978-0-593-61374-0

A Safe House
ISBN 978-0-593-55629-0